Mick Donnellan is a novelist, playwright, and screenwriter. He worked with Druid Theatre and RTE before setting up his own company, Truman Town Theatre. After years of stellar success on stage, his play Radio Luxembourg was optioned and adapted for the screen as Tiger Raid. Shot in Jordan and starring Brian Gleeson, Sofia Boutella, and Damian Molony, it premiered (to critical acclaim) at the Tribeca Film Festival in New York. Galway Blues is Mick's fifth novel. His fiction has won numerous awards, and his other plays are regularly adapted for the national and international screen.

Read more at www.mickdonnellan.com

ALSO BY MICK DONNELLAN

Fiction
El Niño

Fisherman's Blues

The Naked Flame

The Dead Soup

Editor: Tales from the Heart

Plays
Sunday Morning Coming Down

Shortcut to Hallelujah

Gun Metal Grey

Velvet Revolution

Radio Luxembourg

Nally

Checkpoint Charlie

The Crucified Silence

Screen
Tiger Raid

Nally

Lucky Run

Galway Blues

A Novel

by

Mick Donnellan

Best wishes
Mick Donnellan

www.mickdonnellan.com

Copyright © 2024 Mick Donnellan

All rights reserved

The characters and events portrayed in this book are fictitious. Any similarity to real persons, living or dead, is coincidental and not intended by the author.

No part of this book may be reproduced, or stored in a retrieval system, or transmitted in any form or by any means, electronic, mechanical, photocopying, recording, or otherwise, without express written permission of the publisher.

Cover design by: Art Painter
Library of Congress Control Number: 2018675309
Printed in the United States of America

For Nairobi, always.

"Never trust a writer."
Una Lynch.

Nice bitta dusht

Guilt has the sharpest tooth and she was biting down hard. So hard even a whole bottle of Jameson could do nothing to kill the pain. Still, I took another long swill but the bitch just kept on coming, like emotional wet cement turning fast into concrete fear.

Rattle goes the phone, like a room full of tormented skeletons. It was Oscar and he said: 'Last time we met, your liver was about to burst.'

'Where was that?'

'Mill Street Station. I thought you were dead for sure. Are you still drinkin?'

'I am. And busy doin it. What do you want?'

'I've a score on tonight. Will you come?'

He said *score* like he was trying to impress me.

'What is it?'

'We're robbing a few handy places. Nice bitta dusht.'

'How much *dusht*?'

'It'll be decent. The more we steal, the more we make. I'll tell you more when I meet ya.'

'Where'll that be?'

'How's Salthill at eight, across from the casino?'

'I'll be there. Don't forget to steal a car if we're doin a job.'

He hesitated, didn't see that coming, then said: 'No problem.'

I hung up and polished off the Jameson. It sang on my tongue, danced on my tonsils, but didn't get me drunk. Just topped up. Ready to start drinking right.

Thought about another bottle.

Said I'd stay steady for Oscar's thing.

Drink after.

Later in Salthill.

Smell of seaweed.

People walking the prom.

The sun dipping down behind the hungry Atlantic.

Smoked three Benson before Oscar arrived.

He pulled up in a '99 Toyota Starlet.

It looked like a pure ball of shite.

I walked around it, like a food critic looking at botulism.

Oscar let the window down. He had sallow skin. Brazilian roots. I said: 'You're twenty minutes late.'

'Sorry, man. I was finishin a burger at the house.'

Didn't even know where to start with that, sat in, asked: 'Where we goin?'

'Down here. I'll show ya.'

He pulled off in first gear, roaring loud, driving like an old woman late for mass. Couldn't get into second, muttering to himself. I looked around. Screeching wipers. Cigarette butts beside the gearstick and an old bottle of Sprite on the floor.

I asked him: 'Where'd you lamp this fuckin yoke?'

'Father Griffin Road. Wasn't even locked.'

'I'd say twas made long before locks were even invented.'

'Don't worry, it'll do the job.'

We came off the roundabout, headed west, not much out here worth robbing. I lit another Benson, dry on the tongue, chemical burn on the roof of my mouth, popped the question with: 'So where's this place you're on about?'

He pointed to a dark corner in the car park on the left, said: 'See them big metal boxes over there?'

'Yeah?'

'Yeah, well they're fulla clothes.'

'So?'

'So we're goin to rob them and sell the stuff to a warehouse.'

He was trying to sound confident. I waited for the punchline. It didn't come, so I said: 'Are you fuckin serious?'

'There's good money in it.'

'In what? Robbin charity clothes bins?'

'Charity begins at home, man.'

'Go home so. You fuckin gobshite.'

'No need to be a bollox about it. We all need to make a livin somehow.'

That's when I knew this wasn't a real hit.

He was desperate. Winging it. Needed help from someone that knew what the fuck they were doing.

I found some rare patience, asked: 'How'll you even get the stuff out?'

'I've one of my young fellas comin.'

'With what? Somethin to cut the locks?'

'No, we'll have to put him *into* it.'

'*Into* where?'

'We'll lodge him into the clothes bin, the same as if we're

donatin somethin.'

'And?'

He parked the car, or it cut out, I wasn't sure.

'And he can give us the bags from in there.'

'And what if he can't get out?'

His logic was losing cabin pressure now. 'If he can get in, he'll be able to get out.'

'The doors on them things are designed to only go one way.'

'Fuck off, Charlie. I know what I'm doin.'

'Besta luck with it so. I'll get out here.'

'Are ya not comin?'

'I've a few things on. I have to go.'

'Go where?'

'Anywhere but here. I thought you had somethin serious lined up?'

'This is the only way to make money. Unless you go into the drugs. And nobody knows what the fuck's goin on with that crowd. We can start here and set up our own warehouse eventually.'

He looked at me, like a vulnerable dog, hoping this last statement would resurrect his dead self-respect.

I said: 'There's a Topaz petrol station over there.'

Wide eyes. 'Where?'

'There. Look.'

He saw it, said: 'So?'

'Have you a gun?'

'I do.' He said, curious. 'Under the seat.'

'It's not a water pistol now or anythin?'

'It's a fuckin gun. But them places have CCTV, alarm

buttons, shutters, security locks.'

'They also have money. *Cash*.'

He leaned down. Searched. Found it. Held it up. It wasn't too bad. Glock. Good weight, loaded, genuine.

'I've never used it. A fella just threw it over the wall one night when he was runnin from the guards.'

'It'll do the job. You wait in the car outside. Be ready to drive as soon as you see me comin. Can you manage that?'

'I think so, but what are you goin to do?'

'Just park over there.'

'This is mental, Charlie, I don't know.'

'Have you a bag?'

'I've one of the schoolbags from home?'

'It'll do. Pour out what's in it.'

He did. Schoolbooks and copies fell out. It smelled like rotten bananas. The situation was pure ape, but fuck it, I needed the money for drink and it was too late to go robbing anywhere else.

Oscar had a balaclava ready for the big fashion heist. I took that. Put it on. It smelled like wet marshmallow.

'Sure you don't want me to come?' He asked.

'Fuckin positive.' I said. And got out.

Exterior. Galway. Night. Adrenaline.

Walked over, between the pumps and the bags of coal. A liquorice smell of motor oil.

The Prodigy were in my head with *Smack my bitch up*.

The ground became air unbound. My mind in a glorious episode of criminal symmetry. A return to the source. My blood throbbed, my heart danced. The lights of the shop like a supernova.

My vision swayed as I put a hand on the door. Once I was in, that was it.

What were you doing in the shop wearing a balaclava and holding a gun, Charlie?

I was in for a bar of chocolate, your honour.

Like fuck.

Interior. Topaz. Bright and warm. No customers. Radio going with chill music. Closing for the night in sight. Until now. The fella behind the counter was unpacking a box of Tayto. Buck teeth like Roger Rabbit.

His tag said - *Manager: Trevor Jones.*

Early thirties. Brown eyes. Black hair. He looked at the balaclava and the gun, pulled a contorted face, like he just stepped on dogshit, then pressed the security button.

Silent alarm. Three-minute response time. Needed to work fast. Hit him with the butt of the Glock and it cracked his jaw and put him unconscious.

Time to go for the money. I hopped over. Bags of Tayto bursting under my feet.

Could hear myself breathing, like a diver under water.

The till was full of cash. Purple, yellow, blue. Sound.

Stuffed them into my jacket.

Trevor groaned so I gave him a kick to keep him quiet.

The tunes overhead went to Pink Floyd - *Brain Damage.* Crepuscular notes leaning light on the pleasure centres.

Things were looking good, simple, straightforward.

That's when the young one came back from her break. Arrived from a door behind me.

Skinny black jeans. Big arse. Blonde and acne.

The name on her tag said: *Sharon.*

She paused in shock. Looked at her phone. She seemed

conflicted, like she didn't know whether to run or take a video.

She decided to run. Something she wasn't used to. I took my time and shot her in the leg.

The gun had a loud report.

My ears were ringing after it.

Sharon dropped, screamed. Held the wound.

Blood present, stains the floor. The fabric of reality is torn as the shark of death smells a score. Her pain got louder, shriller, more likely to attract unwanted attention from outside. Time to quieten her.

I looked around. Found the fire extinguisher.

Used that.

Belted her over the head.

There was a sound like breaking twigs and she went limp.

I couldn't feel my arms now, my legs. I couldn't feel myself at all. A floating entity of violence, a storm outside your window, waiting to make a kill.

Here's Charlie death, here's a cyclone of hate, drenched in purpose, expertise, and authority.

Opened the schoolbag. Packed away a few boxes of cigarettes.

Lottery tickets.

Coins.

Now time for the drink.

Vodka, whisky, Jack Daniels.

Jameson for dessert.

Then I was 087. Ready to go.

Zipped up the bag.

The door opened and I looked up with a premonition of early guards but it was just a fat fella wanting to pay for petrol.

He was holding a fifty in his hand, stunned at the sight of me.

I walked over, took the fifty, said: 'That's grand, thanks.'

And I walked out.

Sirens already in the distance.

I got to the car. Sat in. Oscar was nervous. 'Did you rob the place?'

'I did. Now drive.'

'Where?'

'Barna. We'll burn the car there.'

'Burn it?'

'It's about all it's good for. Now FUCKIN DRIVE!'

Four kids

One can of petrol. Box of matches. Up she went. Oscar watched the flames and asked: 'Do you want to do the bins tomorrow, so?'

'No, thanks, Oscar.'

He paused in thought, then said: 'I think you're in a much bigger league than me.'

'I don't think you're in any league at all.'

'I saw a picture of your girlfriend. On the paper. The one they raped and killed.'

I took a long swig of whisky, asked: 'Is that right?'

'She was gorgeous. Did you kill Kramer and that detective too?'

'We better go.'

'Is there still a price on your head?'

'Price on my head?'

'Hundred thousand. Did you not know?'

'No. Who's fundin that?'

'Fella called McWard. He's tryin to take over things after Kramer. Nobody really likes him.'

'You mean nobody really fears him. Otherwise, I'd be gone.'

We looked at the fire, then Oscar asked: 'Where are you stayin anyway?'

'Nowhere.'

'You can have the couch at mine if you want. I've four kids, but the couch is free.'

'You're grand, thanks. I'll find a hostel.'

'It'd be an honour, Charlie. Charlie the legend.'

Breaking twigs. Sharon's head. Broken teeth on Trevor Jones.

Charlie, I thought. The fuckin legend.

Deadborn

Interior. Oscar's house. Days later. We'd made €11,000 on the job. Good grade. I'd been staying here since. It was safe and the neighbours minded their own business. The cops kept away too. Last time they were around, someone broke their windshield with a brick and threw a petrol bomb on the roof. Third degree burns and a quiet life since.

Oscar was shaking me to wake up.

'Charlie? *Charlie?*'

'What...Oscar? What?'

'McWard was on the phone.'

'Who the fuck is McWard?'

'He's tryin to take over things. I told ya the other night. Drugs and all that. He has the price on your head. He wants you to ring him.'

I sat up. Looked around. The sun was glaring through the window, bouncing off the empty cans of Heineken on the carpet. The fireplace was full of Supermacs wrappers and used nappies. Screeching kids in the kitchen. A smell like burnt toast. My mouth was dry. Been sweating for hours. Nausea taking over. I found some Jameson on the floor. Pulled the seal, drank it. Burnt my oesophagus and felt great.

Oscar watched me, asked: 'So what'll we do?'

'About what?'

'McWard.'

'It's my head the price is on. What're *you* worried about?'

'I don't know. I don't even know how he got my number. I never even talked to him before. You better call him. You might be able to sort something out.'

Beat.

Then he said: 'Do you want toast?'

'No, thanks.'

The day was coming in like the miserable tide. The *ten-year-old* sat on a chair in the corner. Jet black hair, reading a book. I know he's ten because when Oscar introduced me, he said: 'That's the ten-year-old.'

In the other corner there was a huge television after landing and a small blonde girl was trying to tune it. Controls in her hand, looking at the white noise.

'Any luck, Amy?' Asked Oscar.

She shook her head but stayed focused.

Oscar's woman, her name was Deirdre, came from upstairs and walked into the kitchen.

Her brown hair was in a tight ponytail and she was wearing loose jeans and red shoes. Cratered face and her eyes were bleak, almost black, like she'd been through something dark, her mind beyond reach.

Oscar went out to say something to her and she started complaining about having no money. Her voice was deep, torn, like she'd swallowed cheap razor blades. The kids needed clothes and food. She wanted cigarettes and why did he buy a big stupid telly when they couldn't afford it?

He was trying to tell her he was doing his best, and he robbed a Topaz just for her, and did she not appreciate it?

She told him she'd prefer if he was in jail and she could claim single mothers allowance and not be depending on a retard like him.

He said that hurt his feelings and why did she have to be

so mean?

She told him to fuck off, smashed a cup off the wall, and said if he wanted lodgers in the house, tell them to start paying a bit of rent and not be taking up the couch in the morning when she wants to watch the new big fuckin telly.

The door opened.

He came in and sat down.

I lit a smoke, asked: 'Everythin alright, Oscar?'

'Herself is kickin off.'

'I heard.'

'She used to be sound, y'know. Until…'

'Is she sick?'

'She's strugglin with the heroin. It's not easy. Our last child was deadborn too and ever since she's up and down with the needles. Most of the Topaz score is gone on debts already….and the telly.'

He looked at the ground and thought about that.

I took out my wad of cash. Peeled off a grand and said: 'Here, good man.'

'A grand? For what?'

'Fuck it. It's only money.'

'I can't take this, Charlie.'

'Give it to herself, so. Call it rent.'

He looked at it, then back at me, said: 'Thanks, man. That'll take the heat off for a while.'

'I'll find somewhere else to stay too.'

'You don't have to, like. She's happy once she has a few pound.'

'Shtill, I'll go.'

'What are we goin to do about McWard?'

15

'I'll sort him out.'

He paused, then said: 'Thanks, Charlie.'

'I'll see you around.'

'Let me know if you want to do any more *Topazes*.'

'Keep it down, Oscar. Keep it down.'

'Oh yeah. Shit, sorry.'

'G'luck.'

Prelapsarian Glimpse

Exterior. Outside Oscar's house. Rahoon. His door was light and damp with cracked glass and rusty hinges. I pulled it open and walked into the day. The small lawn was full of long grass and prams and bits of broken slides. On the path there was a dirty puddle with old, scratched lottery tickets and my own fractured reflection.

A chill Atlantic wind blew, shook me like a vindictive demon. My blood in flames like it was full of scorpions and rust. A psychological clamour going on, like my brain was trapped in a death metal concert, double bass, screaming lyrics of despair, unending torture. I needed to take the edge off, bad and fast.

Had the Jameson with me. The last of the stolen booze. Took a long swig. A delight of dancing stars.

Lit a smoke.

Could hear the tobacco burn, felt the tug in my chest, the blast in my windpipe. The Chemical Brothers came from a window, or passing car, or distant glitch in the time-space warp. Took my mind in their grip with *Galvanize.*

"*The time has come to…push the button.*"

A truck roared past, clouds burst, rain came in with urgency and I had nowhere to go. Infinity gripped my heart, squeezed until I nearly blacked out.

Then.

Interior. Brothel. Afternoon.

Brown knee-high boots. Leather skirt.

Her name was Lucy.

I figured this out when she said: 'I'm Lucy.'

Blonde hair in a short ponytail. Looked vaguely Swedish with bright blue eyes. She took my drenched coat and hung it on the door.

Told me to follow her upstairs.

On the way up, it was awful quiet, like a place that used to be a B&B or a parochial house.

She led me to a room at the top. It was large, spacious, and sang secrets of multiple fucks on the bed and the floor and up against the walls. Clothes all over the place. Skirts, tights, underwear. Purple heels. A bedside locker with an ashtray full of smoked joints. A smell like bloody water and warm tar on a road.

Double mattress. We lay down, let the springs sing. She knew my form, what was needed, brought me all the way to ecstatic calm serenity.

After, she hung on, scratched my chest lightly, her head on my shoulder, she said: 'I recognise you. You were with El Niño.'

'I'm payin you to forget.'

'You want to *forget* her?'

'Not her. The pain of life without her.'

'Isn't that a sign of how much you cared? The more pain you're in?'

'I don't know, probably.'

Beat. Then she said: 'And now there's a price on your head.'

'You know about that too?'

'Of course. Everybody knows. Don't worry. You're safe in this place.'

'What's he like?'

'McWard? He comes in but I always refuse him.'

'Why?'

'I don't do the things he wants. The other girls tell me. Really sick.'

'Do you know where he lives?'

'I can find out?'

'Maybe, yeah.'

'I have to go downstairs. Stay a while. Like I said, you're safe.'

'Thanks.'

She studied me, said: 'You have eyes that read books, like the students that come here.'

She got up, lit a scented candle, and left. The room closed in like a warm glove. Her bed was womblike and cosy. Soon my body surrendered and I slept. And slept more.

She came and went a few times.

Probably had other tricks downstairs or around town.

She was there again in the morning, looking at me. A tenderness in her stare, sadness, loss.

Life outside. Birds. Lawnmowers. Innocence. I saw what it could be like to be pure. A prelapsarian glimpse, an alternative world, an eclipse with a parallel universe. A girlfriend, a wife, a lover, a song lamenting from behind a locked door. But then I remembered. And the demons got hold of me, digging in their claws, pulling at my toes, gnawing at my stomach.

A knock on the door, another customer.

She looked at me sadly as the moment died.

Howya, Macky

Got a taxi into town. Driver tried to make small talk, but he gave up after a while. The Killers came through on the radio – *Sam's Town (live from Abbey Road)*. Let that ride, the irony of it. My hand jerked. I felt my brain turn to ice. My legs going weak. And then the crippling fear, like an evil siren in the distance, getting closer all the time.

The taxi cost €11.80.

Gave him €20.

Didn't wait for the change.

Got out on Eyre Square. Raining again, honest weather, my type of world, no fucking around. My mouth watered when I saw The Harvest off-licence, like a toy shop for drinkers. I walked over, like Mick Jagger with the wild horses. Stepped over a homeless fella on the way in, unsure if he was dead or asleep.

Interior. Drink everywhere. Smell of cardboard. Bright lights. Fridges to the right with frosted doors. Lots of wine from various countries. Lad behind the counter is tall with short hair and looks bored. He's got an Australian accent, talking to a girl in front of me buying a naggin of vodka. She wants Grey Goose, talking like the taste matters.

I scanned the stash behind him. Jim Beam called out to me, like we needed a long chat.

The girl leaves. Just me and the kangaroo. I say: 'Bottle of Jimmy.'

'Jim Beam, eh? Too easy.'

He swings round, pulls it down. Lands it in front of me,

says: '€29.80.'

Looks me in the eye for the first time and falters. Goes to my shoes and works his way up.

'Bad day, eh?'

I shrug. Hand him the grade. The bottle in my hand. This is where the wolf meets the man and we become one. The drunk energy seeping through the bag, electrifies my palm.

He gives me the change, says: 'Cheers, mate.'

Exterior. Eyre Square. Day. There was a man from Ballinrobe once who talked a lot about drinking. He used to say: 'When I'm drinkin, I can't understand people that *don't drink*, and when I'm sober, I can't understand people that *do*.'

This is what I thought about as I sat on the steps and unscrewed the cap. I'm not sure which is the more pleasurable. The seconds before the drink, or the glory after. It does the Riverdance in my mouth. Hits all the buds simultaneously. Flows down my oesophagus like euphoric acid. Gushes into my stomach like welcome lava. I pull back, rasp and wince. Almost topple over.

Now El Niño's voice grazes across my delicate mind. A girl passing, the way she talks, something she says, marries the memory. A gentle push, an affectionate whisper. A fragment of our time, some lost lyric of our fading tune, then the echo of my name in her soft lament. Suddenly she's afraid. *Charlie?* She's saying. *Where are you, Charlie?* Over and over again.

An infinite loop, a rose-coloured angelus of torment.

Closed my eyes, shook my head until the chasm subsided. Opened up with a sense of regained control. Directed the grief into bitterness and rage. Even let out a shout, a deep wounded yelp. This is why drunks talk to themselves, roar in public. We're at war, pushing down the shame of all that haunts us.

Took another swig and her voice died down, but wasn't gone, just numbed with the blast. Reached into my pocket for smokes. Found a yellow piece of paper. Neat handwriting. Lucy had written McWard's address for me. He was in an apartment block down by the docks.

Something to do, somewhere to go.

Exterior. Outside McWard's. Grey sky. Boats. Swans squealing.

His name was on the buzzer on a brown door. Second floor.

Mr. Incognito.

I buzzed. No answer.

Waited until a girl came along and let herself in with a fob and I followed her. She was holding a bag of tayto and a bar of chocolate. Gave me a curious look going up the mouldy stairs but said nothing.

Found the turn to McWard's place and cut her loose.

Green painted hallway. Torn red carpet. A bored draught, ghosts, atoms, the unknown song.

His door was made of cheap wood that was hollow when I knocked.

Nobody answered, even though I could hear voices inside. So I went again, louder this time. The interior tones went quiet, and the door slowly opened. The hinges groaned and there was a smell like turpentine. The guy was wearing a tracksuit, tight hair, earring. Looked like he was in a boyband for mongs. He scanned me up and down, then shouted back: 'There's a fella here, Macky.'

Macky.

There was a muffled and annoyed shout back.

Then the mong said: 'He's in the jacks. C'mon in.'

Timber floor. Smell of weed and rotten meat and unwashed sheets. Dark, like no light during the day through foggy windows. Low beats dance music playing in the background. A fat girl on a bean bag scrolling through a smartphone.

More scumbuckets sitting on the couch, scratching themselves, their eyes bright with the reflection of the big television in the corner. All entranced by a video game.

They must have thought I was there to buy drugs, or deliver pizza, but there was no pizza, so it had to be drugs.

A toilet flushed down the hall. The handle creaked on another cheap door and McWard emerged. Flooded the place with a smell of shite like slurry mixed with cheap wine.

He had short black hair and chubby hands. Breezed by me towards the couch and sat down. Big belly and runners, and loose blue jeans, wearing a Scarface t-shirt, Pacino on the front, holding a gun and saying the famous quote.

He picked up a controller and started pressing buttons.

I lit a smoke and said: 'Howya, Macky.'

He looked over, realised it was me, then pulled a face like his mother just caught him wanking.

'Jesus! What the fuck are you doin *here?*'

The rest of them looked up like they expected the real Jesus, their necks going back and over like demented emus.

'I heard you were lookin for me.'

Silence fucked around. Somewhere between reverence and fear.

Then McWard said: 'Yeah, Charlie. Eh, call me Larry. Sit down, good man.'

'I won't, thanks.'

He looked across the couch, at his useless crew and said: 'Give us the room, lads.'

'Are you sure?' Asked the mong.

'Yeah. Go on.'

They got up, slow and lazy. Anchored with thoughts about how to exist in the outside world.

The fat one looked up at me from the bean bag, then back at McWard, asked: 'Me too?'

'You too, Sharon. Go on.'

'Do I have ta?'

'Fuck off will ya?'

'Don't be such a prick.'

'Go down there and get me a curry chips.'

'With what? I'm not fuckin loaded.'

'Here's €50.'

She stomped over, took it and stormed out.

Conflict gathered her thoughts now, got ready for the drama, and then we began.

'Well, what can I do for ya?'

'You've a price on my head. Why?'

The colour went from his face. He looked around for something. I thought he might be going for a weapon, so I took out Oscar's Glock and hit the table with a decent thud.

He bent down and found a pack of smokes and lit up, inhaled hard, composed himself, exhaled towards the ceiling, like he was judging me from a pedestal of power.

'I used to work for Kramer. It seemed like the honourable thing to do.'

I thought about that, said: 'It won't bring him back.'

'Why'd you do him? Everythin was goin great.'

'Who said it was me?'

'It was because of your burd. Little Gino.'

'El Niño.'

'That's her. I was sorry to hear she died.'

'You weren't sorry. You didn't give a fuck.'

'You're right. I didn't. But it's important to make a point when a boss gets killed. People need to know there's consequences. Another thing, I heard you did a place the other night, out by Salthill.'

'What's your point?'

'I'm taxin jobs around the city. Nobody told me you were goin robbin.'

'Why would they? I didn't even know who the fuck you were until two days ago.'

'Well now you know. Are you not impressed?'

'I'm overwhelmed.'

'I won't tax you this time.'

'That's kind of you.'

'Let you off with a caution. If you want to keep up the good work, then I'll call off the contract on your head too.'

'You should know I'm not a big fan of tax either way.'

'Nobody is, Charlie, but things are changin. This is my city now.'

'It's a sign of weakness.'

He didn't like that, sat up and the couch squeaked under the pressure. 'What do you mean?'

'Tryin to force respect like that. It won't work.'

'What would you know?'

'I grew up with Kramer, worked with him for years. Watched him eliminate Max and all the other fuckheads around the country that thought they had form. He had what it takes.'

'And I don't?'

'Not from what I've seen.'

'You haven't seen much.'

'How long's the price been on my head?'

'Three weeks.'

'And nobody's popped me yet? With Kramer they'd have done it in an hour for free. Then they'd dig me up a week later and shoot me again, just for pleasure.'

'I could do you right now.'

'But you won't. That's the problem. And if you tried, I'd put you through that dirty window in a matter of seconds. And nobody would give a fuck, except the misfortunate street cleaners that had to clean your fat fuckin hole off the footpath.'

He pointed the cigarette, said: 'I'm doublin that price tonight.'

'Triple it. Won't make any difference. People respect me for what I did. What have you done? Played computer games?'

'I'm in charge.'

'In charge of what? You think you're in charge because nobody else has took over. They're waiting for the cops to calm down.'

'I'm just puttin all my ducks in a row. A month from now, I'll have everythin back to normal.'

'It's a power vacuum. The only fuckin duck here is you and you won't last. You'll be wiped out in a matter of weeks.'

'Oh really, and what then, genius?'

'And then I'll be worried. G'luck.'

And I left.

Fuckin eejit.

Phantom Perfume

Lucy had me going about the books.

Decided to hit the college. Students everywhere. Figure that.

Almost a year since I finished my degree. Came in through the Access Programme.

They said I deserved a chance at an education.

I got that alright.

Hit the library. People smoking outside. Walked in. It was busy. Lots of fellas with fuzzy hair talking Irish.

Got to the Arts Section.

Looked around the shelves for something decent.

Read the first pages of a few: Sartre, Camus, Umberto Eco, Ishiguro.

Lost interest after a while, like a priest with no faith.

Took a walk around. Through the mist of brighter memories. Met El Niño on my last day here. I could feel her now. Her essence in every fibre of the place. Phantom perfume, a laugh from upstairs. Walking where she had walked, touching what she had touched. I loved her then, I love her now. I loved her before I even knew her. I felt split in two. Here but detached. Could see myself from the far side of the room. Greyed out from the colour, etching out a condemned existence. There's a name for it. Dislocation. Something like that.

Kept going through the shelves, like the invisible man, no real plan. The sun blasting through the window like a diamond on fire. Another Galway season in one day. My shirt was tight on my skin as I got the smell of papyrus down by the Economics. Marx gave me a strange look from the spine of *Das Kapital*. Howya, Karl.

The Jim Beam was wearing off. Time to top up soon. Came around by the study area. Laptops left abandoned. Smartphones on top of wallets in front of empty desks. Helped myself to a few of them. A pink purse. A black leather bulger full of credit cards and cash. Probably rent. Or the grant, or daddy's weekly instalment. All sweetly in my pocket like micro-dopamine hits. Thought about stealing a MacBook but it'd be too much hassle to sell.

And your one that owned it was a ride.

Started getting looks from the porters, from suspicion to recognition.

Time to go before I got careless.

Went down the stairs. Through the lobby.

Outside, surrounded by careless youth, it was like freedom and sadness. So much possibility. All impossible. I took a seat on a bench under a tree. The air was cool, gentle, and understanding.

My hands were shaking with delirium tremens and adrenaline. Went through the contraband. Her licence, his student ID.

She was Emily.

He was Graham.

She was blonde with bright green eyes.

He had tousled hair and a ciabatta look, like pint bottles of cider and rugby in the pub on a Saturday.

Receipts and loyalty cards for chemists and hair salons.

A gym membership.

All their cash.

€275 in total.

I took that and dropped the rest on the path where it could easily be found.

The credit cards were tempting but not worth it. Last fella I knew that tried that went to buy a snack box in Supermacs and ended up getting caught on the CCTV and it was broadcast on *CrimeCall*.

Time to go. Thirst and need taking hold. A prick with funky glasses was talking on the phone about going to the college bar.

So I took it as a sign and went there.

Promise of escape

Interior. College bar. Day. A smell like gravy and garlic bread. And beer drenched beermats. Blackboard to the right announcing cider on special offer. Ordered myself some of that.

Fella behind the counter called was called John. He left it down, like a promise of escape. It was cold and saturated in luscious condensation. Full to the brim like a perfect thing. I drank it like an expert and broke it in two. Didn't spill a precious drop. It went down smooth and calm and tasted good, like silk and sugar. I could do this all day and do it right.

The Smiths on the speakers with *Every Day Is Like Sunday.* Plays on the nerves, surfs the bloodstream, taps into the underlying mechanisms, ropes the chaos into order. John looked over, asked: 'Want another?'

I did. He filled it and I paid him with a crispy stolen twenty. Took my change, and the television caught my eye. News on. They were looking for witnesses to the Topaz robbery.

Had me on camera.

There's Charlie walking out.

Leather jacket and balaclava. That ball of shite Toyota pulling away.

Good thing Oscar had stolen it.

The reporters weren't taking too kindly to Sharon's condition, either.

Bullet wound to the knee.

Cracked skull.

Life support.

Crying family.

The usual.

I had another long wallop of the pint, let it swirl before it sank down, like a glorious army, destroying the concern taking hold. What if she died? Could Oscar handle it?

A flashback of Lucy came like a welcome distraction. Caught her scent on the back of my hand. Another night with her could be ok. A warm night of fuckin and drinking and thinking about nothing. And nothing happening. Only the stars in the sky and her legs like a road to forget.

Then, like a predator with prey, I spotted a wallet behind the counter. Cash sticking out the sides. Probably belonged to John.

Did I need it?

No.

Would I pass up an opportunity?

Fuck no. I had no choice, your honour. It's all I'm good at. Built into the genes.

John was busy with the dishwasher. Perfect timing. I leaned over and went for the grab. Next thing I felt a hand on my shoulder. Definitely a bouncer. He went: 'What the fuck do you think you're doin?'

And he threw me out the door.

Freddie

Later on the prom, drowning my sorrows. The stunt at the college had cost me half a pint. That's the problem with drinking slow, ya never know when things are going to kick off. I should've known better.

Bought myself a bottle of Buckfast, sat on a bench facing the ocean and went slugging away, watching the swans, and the crusty types on the beach playing guitar and rolling joints and talking about different festivals and bands. After a while, I could feel eyes watching me, like curious heat. When you're at this level of dead humanity, you're down to the bare limbic functions. The cognitive side is frazzled and you're living on animal instinct. I spotted a Mondeo across the road, parked in the bus stop like a pure wank. The driver smiling at me from inside. Then he gets out and walks over. I'm thinking if he asks me for a blowjob, I'll break his jaw.

He took shape. I recognised him from years ago.

Freddie someone, from somewhere.

Black leather jacket, fuzzy hair.

Jaundiced teeth and eyes the colour of jaded old newspaper.

He opened up, with: 'Howya, Charlie.'

'I'm only fuckin middlin, Freddie.'

'You weren't done for the double murder down in Ballinrobe yet?'

'I don't know what you're talking about.'

'I heard they had no proof and had to let you go?'

'Is there somethin ya wanted?'

'I need a favour.'

'What kind?'

'Come on up to the house.'

'Where's the house?'

'Claremont Park. Not far.'

'I'm busy.'

'Busy drinkin?'

'It's a full-time job.'

'I've plenty of booze up there if ya want it.'

'Now you're makin sense.'

Interior. Freddie's house.

Torn linoleum, antiquated world.

Cans of paint under the stairs.

A smell like wet grass.

Star newspaper on the kitchen table, beside a full ashtray.

Dirty fridge. Stained cups left around with mouldy tea bags still inside them.

He went to a press, handed me a bottle of Jim Beam.

Just in time, I was only after finishing the Bucky.

I cracked it open. Bought into the bourbon security.

Freddie sat down, put his back to the wall.

Black jeans. Black boots, loose laces. Wiry fucker.

He lit a smoke, rolled up shite. The lighter fell on the table with an echo of light wood.

'People are afraid of you now, you know?'

'How'd you find me?'

'You rode one of my whores.'

'Should she not be practicing client confidentiality?'

'She said nothin. I saw you walkin out. And the bouncer at the college works for me too.'

'You're well known, so?'

'Not as well as you. I thought you were still down in Ballinrobe?'

I took a hit of the JB, drowned out the flashbacks I didn't want, said: 'Came back up for a change of scenery.'

'Like what? The inside of a Topaz?'

'So I'm doin a few scores, what the fuck's it to you?'

'Nothin to me. I was laughing when I seen it on the news. I says: *"There's fuckin Charlie on the telly."* That's how I knew you were back around.'

There was a motorbike in the garden. Flames on the side, bright red and newly painted. Asked him: 'Where'd you get the bike?'

'My oul fella. He died on it. Fuckin brakes went.'

'What is it?'

'Suzuki. Perfect for doin jobs.'

'Like what? Deliverin pizzas?'

He got serious then, hint of anger. 'Don't do that, Charlie.'

'What?'

'Disrespect my dead father's bike.'

Sparked a smoke. It tasted like confidence and authority and time to think, asked: 'So what kind of work are you into?'

'The ordinary kind.'

'What's that mean?'

'No drugs.'

'Why not?'

'The jail time ain't worth the money.'

'Were you not in Kramer's crew?'

'I left soon after you. Went out on my own. Pullin strokes.'

'What kinda strokes?'

'Handy ones. Type of stuff you'd be good at yourself. I have all the brothels, bouncin, debt collectin. Nice cash earners that don't interest the drugs squad, but worth the same money.'

Dragged hard, asked: 'What do you make of this fella *McWard*?'

'Waste of space, but handy to have him there.'

'How so?'

'Keeps the cops busy watchin him.'

'He has a price on my head.'

'Hundred grand, I heard about it.'

'Anyone I should be worried about?'

'No, it's a joke. Everyone thinks he's a tool. He thought puttin the bounty on you would show people he's serious about running a gang but I wouldn't put him in charge of a lemonade stand.'

'So who's really takin over?'

'The drugs? I dunno yet. Don't care. Like I said: ain't worth the money. Some people say there's politicals interested, others reckon Kramer had a thing with a crowd of Croatians. Then there's the Travellers in the middle of all that. Fuck them, they can have it.'

We let the kindred air settle, the silence speak, then I said: 'You mentioned a favour?'

'I did. Do you want to make a handy few pound?'

'Doin what?'

'I need a van collected tonight in Loughrea.'

'What's in it?'

'Smuggled cigarettes.'

'Why you offerin it to me?'

'Man with your skills, and expertise and fear factor, I could do with you. If it works out, there could be a few more like it. Call it a tester to see how we get on.'

'Where in Loughrea?'

'Out by the Plaza. It'll be left down by the petrol pumps.'

'How'll I get there?'

'You'll have to steal a yoke. And not a shitebox of a Starlet this time.'

'Funny fucker.'

'I'll lend you a few tools.'

'What's the wages for this?'

'Will €500 keep you happy?'

'It's a start.'

Paddy lugs

Freddie gave me a bag of useless scrap to rob a car. Pliers. Clothes hangers. Hammers. A tablet for the immobiliser. I threw it all in a skip on Dominic Street. Walked to Eyre Square. Stood on the corner by the station car park. Smoky fog filled light. Trains hissing in the distance. Waited under the shadow of the streetlight, watching the raindrops dance, and the couples walking by with their jackets over their heads.

Checked out an Insignia, a Mercedes, even an Audi SUV. Decided on a black Volkswagen Passat and got going. Up through Bohermore and faced for the motorway.

Nice wheels. Style, not too flashy or loud, good speed if there was a chase. Pure clean. A smell like peach schnapps, smooth on the road, calm surge. The seats were almost new. The steering like it had never been used. All the buttons were fresh and sensitive. No sensors flashing on the dash. Headlights in perfect working order.

Got to the Dublin exit and hit the M6. Loughrea would take twenty minutes. That's the great thing about the motorway. Cuts out all the bullshit. No more awkward small towns with bad roads. Just in and out. You could be robbing country houses and back in Galway in less than half an hour with a boot full of contraband. You'd even have it sold by the time the guards heard there was a raid.

Trick is not to overdo it. Hit a place *once* and be gone. I knew a fella before, Paddy Lugs they called him, his fuckin ears were massive, robbed the same village three times in the one night. He'd go back into town and offload what he stole and drive out again for more.

A farmer tried to shoot him on the last run. Paddy even showed me the scar where the shotgun pellets had grazed his eye. He was thinking about suing but ended up in jail a week later. Was going hitting the same place *again* but this time the cops were out and he ran the checkpoint with a stolen car and nearly killed a sergeant. Worse again, he crashed up the road and tried to escape on foot. They eventually caught him running across the fields and sent him down for six years. The papers had a great laugh with headlines like: "*Six EARS for Paddy Lugs.*"

Not much traffic tonight. Overtook a Ford Fiesta doing forty. Big L plate on the back window. A constipated lad driving with his head stuck to the windscreen, two hands gripped tight on the wheel. I put him out of sight, got back to the serene darkness and turned up the radio. John Creedon was on with *Intro* by The xx and it suited the scene well.

Swung a left for Loughrea off the Bulaun exit. Got to the Plaza. Bright lights and busy. Trucks. Bewley's coffee. Supermacs. Abba blasting into the forecourt from a tinny speaker with *Dancing Queen*, like buying fuel was a big celebration. Rolled down the window to have a better look for the van. Felt the ancient chill of rural Ireland, bleak in the black distance, an infinity of drizzle and agrarian solitude, poisoned and corrupted by thieves like me, like social discharge called progress or pus.

I found it beside a Texaco lorry. White Ford Transit. Nicely out of sight.

Pulled in. Let things settle and watched through the mirrors. No sign of cops, or unusual cars, or anyone taking notice. I got out, greeted by the unique Galway breeze. It envelops you, looks for a way in, clings to your skin like friendly plastic film.

Freddie said the keys were under the front wheel on the

right.

They weren't.

They were under the back wheel on the far side, damp and keenly cold, as I opened up the cab and got in.

There was a smell of farts and cheese and rhubarb. *Irish Independent* on the dash. Threw it out the window and turned the ignition. It came to life with a grumpy diesel roar. I gave it a minute to find rhythm, our needs to align, then put her in first and faced for Galway.

Cyanide

Back down the dark road. Stopped at a rest area to check out the stash. Had to make sure I could trust Freddie. Most guards won't waste their time following around cigarettes but if it's Semtex, crystal meth or guns, then they're on you like the paparazzi.

The van doors opened with a rusty groan.

Inside, there was a wall of stacked rectangular boxes, like gold bars made from nicotine. I opened a sleeve of Benson. Pulled out a twenty pack. Sparked one. Tasted good, but different, like a generic soft drink. Then I remembered stories about rat poison, cyanide and chemicals that crystallise in your lungs like broken glass. So I let the smoke drift into the Galway air and threw the rest away. Looked around. It was quiet, like dead silence, the night a desert of unspoken things.

A ghostly bus sped past, leaving a swirl of toxic exhaust in its wake. No sign of the law. If they were going to make a move, they'd have to do me now or go the wrong way up the motorway to turn around.

Rang Freddie outside Oranmore. He answered with: 'How'd you get on?'

'On the way back. Where am I goin?'

'D'you know the McDonalds in Rahoon?'

'I do.'

'Leave her outside there and we'll take care of it.'

'When do I get paid?'

'Gimme a shout tomorrow. Where you stayin tonight?'

'Don't know yet.'

'Go down to the brothel and tell them I said it's ok.'

'Better than a park bench I suppose.'

'I'll tell Lucy to expect you.'

Perfume ephemeral, blue eyes, her warm bed.

'You lookin for anythin else, workwise?'

'Like what?'

'How would you be fixed for a bitta bouncin? I've a place on Forster Street. I need security for it. Last fella was ridin too many women and I had to let him go.'

'What's the roubles like?'

'I'll take well care of you. Drop in tomorrow night around eight and I'll get you set up.'

'Do I not need a licence?'

'I'll sort that, don't worry. How'd you get to Loughrea?'

'In a Volkswagen Passat.'

'Did you use the tablet? Was it any good for the immobiliser?'

'Not worth a shite.'

'You hardly broke the window with the hammer?'

'What the fuck would I do that for?'

'Clothes hangers?'

'No.'

He paused, confused, then asked: 'How'd you rob it so?'

'I followed the driver and stole the keys.'

Pause, then: 'Aragh fuck off.'

And he hung up.

The lights of the city were bright like an imminent galaxy. Hit the roundabout and went in by the Galway Clinic. Went by

Renmore and turned left at The Huntsman. Pulled out a naggin. Sipped on that, the vodka burned like reassurance. Turned up the radio. Creedon was banging with Spirit – *Mechanical World.*

Brought the van to Rahoon. Seen the big Arches for McDonalds and parked it there. Kids fucked around outside. Young lads on bikes causing trouble, doing wheelies, trying to impress young girls drinking smoothies and vaping.

I got out, put on my cap and walked into the night. There was a smell like grease and chips and cucumber. Reminded me of childhood and I don't know why. Walked towards the University. My hands were cold in my jacket pockets and my feet felt numb. Did a mental count. €500 for this. Not much, but plenty when your needs are small. On top of the Topaz grade, should keep me going for a while. And it was easier than robbing shops. Only a fraction of the hassle. No guns, no threats, no shooting Sharon types in the knees.

Later, on Shop Street, the drink was feeling redundant, like I drank myself sober. But the night was young, and full of too much rain and time to think. So I went to Lucy's and let her blue eyes sing and her blonde hair cut through the torment and eventually I managed to sleep.

The Galway Hooker

David Bowie *New Killer Star.* The first chords touch, caress, persuade, resurrect something. A snake charmed maybe, a reminder of when. Ordered a pint of Guinness in the Bunch of Grapes. Open fire and the reassuring smell of coal and hot whisky and soup.

The despair was getting me down more than usual. I was getting black flashes of something, like my mind was doing a bungee jump into a dark hole and not always securely tied. Could be a wet brain job. Charlie the vegetable, getting nappies changed in a nursing home somewhere. Not the kinda dramatic exit I'm looking for.

The tips of my fingers were tingling, and the muscles in my legs were throbbing like someone was playing the bongo on my calves. My eyelids kept fluttering and my chest was thumping with an uneven gallop, like the lights flickering before a power cut. This is how my system tells me I need more drink, fast. It won't solve the problems, but it'll mask them long enough to pretend they're not there. And sure what more do you want?

I crippled the pint and opened the *Galway Advertiser* left on the counter. There was a piece about local crime. It talked about new local gangs trying to set up routes, shipments, criminal syndicates. That probably meant McWard. But the other more powerful outfits around the country had been taking advantage of the disorder and were *"muscling in"* and it was causing concern for the guards. No warning they were coming. No resistance from McWard. No tax. No respect whatsoever.

Times like this I missed Kramer. His brutal style. These were circumstances that would inspire a bloodbath. Worse still, he would have never allowed it to come to this in the first place.

I pushed the paper aside and went out for a smoke.

Exterior. Shop Street. Gentle breeze. A fella outside the pub with dreadlocks, pulling on a rolled-up cigarette, talking to a girl drinking a pint of water. Everyone walking by dolled up for the night in style, opulence and expectation. Busker in the distance singing Leonard Cohen, *Famous Blue Raincoat.* It came under me like a spiritual draft, the whole scene a snapshot of Galway's social poetry, a quantum glimpse of paradise. I checked my watch. Eight o'clock. Time to go bouncing. Went back to finish my pint and hit the road.

The place was called *The Galway Hooker.* Between Centra and Rabbite's on Forster Street. Cally was the head doorman. Average height, made of concrete, champion boxer. He had the earpiece and was chewing on gum when I arrived. Galway city accent, east side, all gravel and sand, he said: 'Just keep the cool, any problems let me know.'

Inside was a throb of drinkers. Heineken types with smartphones. Wine merchants and garlic bread efforts. Pop music going and golf on a big screen. Clatter of glasses and stools on wood, and laughter. It was the hum of chaos, human electrons banging together and making sound waves and hassle-free social ripples.

My job was to keep the drunk dickheads out. Stag nights, hen nights, gimps from Dublin and mongs from around the town. A few of the locals knew me.

Howya, Charlie, all that.

A week passed. Handy enough. €300 a night and a few nixers on the side. Stealing a purse out of an open bag. Change left on the counter. Easy wallets. The routine meant I drank less too, gave the body a break from the recent typhoon of self-abuse.

Inside, we had to keep an eye on the staff. Make sure they weren't hassled. Especially Karena. Cally said she was an actor. Working in the bar between gigs, but that's all he knew. Nice chest in the tight black top. Long black hair. Oval face, piercing blue eyes. Sparkling magnetism. Fellas at the bar always trying the case. Buying her drink, asking her out, trying to give her lifts home. She knew how to handle them. Polite but firm, swatted them away with a fast comeback or a gentle refusal. I was kept busy throwing out lads that thought they still had a chance. They'd hide in the toilet, or out in the smoking section, until everyone was gone and then appear like ninjas. Wondering could they have a late drink and Karena's number.

It wasn't long before we got together. It happened simple enough. She needed a way home. The summer was live, and it was always bright, but her house was in Salthill, and the taxi would cost too much. So I borrowed Cally's BMW and gave her a lift.

We were cruising through Shantalla, letting the dawn come and punish the bruised clouds. Her in blue jeans with her hair down, like a long shiny mane, and her claddagh ring, with the heart pointing out, and her pink painted nails, and powerful perfume, like scented opium.

She asked: 'Where you from anyway?'

'Ballinrobe.'

'I knew that.'

'Why'd you ask?'

'I wanted to see if you'd lie.'

'Why would I lie?'

Her accent was full of Galway divilment, like soft holy purity and kind accusation. 'Fellas are always lying.'

'How'd you know where I was from?'

'You're the new bouncer. We're the bar girls. We find these things out.'

I lit a smoke, asked: 'You a Galway girl?'

'Born and bred. I grew up in Lenaboy.'

'What's this about you being an actor?'

Flirty, false surprise, she said: 'So you've been askin around about me too?'

'Professional curiosity. I think you look like Audrey Hepburn.'

'Are you trying to flatter me into sleeping with you?'

'I think you're star quality. Ask anyone at the pub to describe the girls working there. The only one they'll remember is *you*.'

She crossed her thin legs, said: 'Aren't you the silver-tongued charmer.'

'I say it how I see it. Any big films you're in?'

'I don't like talking about myself. You'll just have to google me.'

'Fuck that. Tell me somethin.'

'No. Stop.'

'G'wan.'

She bit her lip, said: 'I'm developing a new screenplay. Set here in the city.'

'What's it about?'

'I'm not allowed to discuss it.'

'Why not?

'I sold it to a production company, and they put an NDA on it.'

'What's that?'

'Non-Disclosure Agreement. The story needs to be locked down for maximum effect when it's released.'

'So you're a writer too?'

'Yes, this is a special project, close to my heart.'

'Will you have a part in it?'

'It needs to get made first, but hopefully. I think you'd like it.'

'Why?'

'It's *crimey*. And sad.'

'Why would I like *crimey*?'

'Seriously?'

'Fair enough. Let me know if you're lookin for any extras.'

She giggled, said: 'Funny guy.'

We came through the lights at Taylor's Hill. 'How far's your house?'

'Do you know Devon Park? It's just up here around the corner.'

'You live alone?'

She gave it a second, let the tone of the question settle, said: 'Yeah. I don't do housemates.'

We let the car hum, the pistons sing, and the engine purr. Then she asked: 'Do you think Cally will want his car back before tomorrow?'

'Probably.'

'That's a pity.'

'Why?'

'I was going to invite you in.'

'You could have any lad you want. Why me?'

'You fishing for compliments?'

'No. Maybe.'

'You're the only one that hasn't tried.'

'I could pull over right now.'

'I want a shower first. You should ring Cally.'

Hers was the last house in Devon Park. Number seven down the back. There, she ran the water, disappeared inside the bathroom. I sat on the bed, took it all in, like analysing the set on the stage before the performance. Books on the floor. Stella Adler. Uta Hagen, Brecht, Caryl Churchill. Marina Carr. A writing desk with a grey laptop and a manuscript beside it. Probably her screenplay. A smell like coconut. Her make-up desk scattered with half used lipstick and jars of expensive looking creams. The window open, the warm June coming in, the birds singing, the rising sun. The door opened and she came out, wrapped in a towel, her hair wet. She walked over and we got into it. Let the summer air drench the room. She was different than she was at work. Her guard down, like she'd been holding herself back. A degree of abandon she refused to show the customers, and that's what drove them wild.

Her breasts were soft and full, her back a smooth glean of perfection. Her climax a tender shudder. Short yet infinite. A silent passing of a great moment, the last second turning on an epoch of history, a moment between metamorphosis, a careening fall toward an angelic glide.

Even when we were spent, she sat astride me still. Her mouth warm on my neck, her tame breathing, her nails on my shoulder blades, our friction smooth from sweat and juices and passion. Trapped in the moment like statues frozen, afraid to wake up, afraid to let time start her count again.

Later, she was curled up naked and asleep. There was a bottle of red wine on the window. I had a swig but didn't need it. Left it back and lit a smoke, listened to Karena's soft breathing, let the meditative rhythm catch my thoughts. Somewhere in the abyss a large hand moved forward, and the past died a bit more, and the day was something new, like the first effects of an experimental cure.

Bitta Debt Collecting

Freddie rang, said: 'Cally reckons you're doin great with the bouncin. I've a couple of more jobs goin if you're interested?'

'Like what?'

'Would you do a bitta debt collectin?'

'From who?'

'There's a politician that owes me money.'

'What for?'

'Does it matter?'

'Not really.'

'I'll call you tomorrow with the address.'

'Sound.'

'Have you seen Karena?'

She was still beside me in the bed. Peaceful, warm, I said: 'No. Why?'

'Cunt never turned up today.'

And he hung up.

She opened her eyes, said: 'Did he just call me *that*?'

'Says you're supposed to be workin?'

'Wanker. He'll get over it.'

She rubbed the sleep from her eyes, said: 'I have a writing deadline anyway. *The Galway Hooker* will have to survive without me.'

She yawned, warm skin, long eyelashes, desire

intoxicated, said: 'And we're not supposed to sleep with other staff, bad for business he says, whatever that means.'

'I'll talk to him.'

She put her hand over my bare chest. 'I really enjoyed last night. I woke up earlier thinking *something good happened*. And then I remembered. And I turned around and you're still here.'

'I'll have to go soon.'

'Debt collecting? I heard that too. Is there anything *not dodgy* about Freddie?'

'Fuck all. I think the pub is legit.'

'Legit? That's a good one. Everyone knows it's a front for money laundering. Does he think people are stupid?'

'What do you mean?'

'The vodka is bootlegged moonshine from the North. Half the kegs are stolen from other bars, and he pays us in cash. No payroll, no records. And all the bouncers have shady backgrounds too…'

'Does that bother ya?'

'I think it's hot.'

And she pulled me closer.

Primal fear

Exterior. Galway. The next day. Time for some debt collection. Kill the day. Hard work doing nothing. Even for alcoholic criminals.

The politician's name was Michael Bell. He had an office on Middle Street. I watched it from across the road. Nice and quiet. No sign of him yet, so I got a bag of cans and a half bottle of Powers. Threw them back and felt fortified. The cider massaging my blood, the Powers soothing my brain. My heart slowed down and I felt pure fire in my nerves, like nervous excitement, abnormal energy. The eradication of civilised thought. It didn't take him long to show up in his shiny new Mercedes. He got out with his paunch and tight navy pants. Black shoes and sleeveless white shirt. Looked like a sex tourist just back from Thailand. He stood outside the office, shoved his hands down his pants and adjusted his balls, then walked in. I gave it a few minutes, drank another can, and followed.

There was a sign on the door that said: **No SalesPeople.**

Then. Interior. Office. Files on the wall. The whir of an antiquated computer with a mouse and a big monitor. A smell like varnish and soap. A woman with short blonde hair and contempt for the general public. Had the look of someone called Dorothy. She was sitting at the desk, staring at the screen. Probably playing solitaire. She noticed me, sighed, and walked over, scanned me up and down, said: 'Yes?'

'Is Michael in?'

Snappy, she asked: 'Why?'

'I want to talk to him.'

Sarcasm, with: 'About?'

'It's a private matter.'

'Can I take a message?'

'You can take a walk inside and tell him I'm *here*.'

Shrill, matter-of-fact, end of the matter, she said: 'But he's not here.'

'His car's outside.'

Surprise now, incredulity. 'How would *you* know his *car*?'

'I do see him drivin around.'

'Well. Now. I'm afraid…'

'You better be afraid. I don't have much patience.'

'Excuse me? I don't know where you think you are but…'

'I know exactly where I am. Do you?'

For the first time she showed doubt, bit her lip and considered the landline on the desk, said: 'I'm not sure you're welcome here.'

That's when I saw the door behind her, with Bell's name written in big black writing, so I pushed her out of the way and went in.

He was on the phone. Hollywood producer style, leaning back on a comfortable office chair, admiring the view out the window. He swung around and frowned. His whole expression said: *something wrong here, something amiss in the way things should be.*

Dorothy was making hysterical noise behind me. I closed the door in her face and locked it.

Bell hung up and stuttered: 'Arr…arr…are you alright there?'

'Sound, thanks. Have you the money you owe Freddie?'

He stood up, unsure. Wondering if there was an angle, some shite he could talk.

'Oh? Freddie, eh, yeah. I mean, no. Hang on, what's this about?'

'You know well what it's about.'

The mask slipped, the local political fame and confidence disappeared. He stood up, said: 'I need more time.'

That's when I took out the Glock and his whole demeanour changed, like I was a doctor with a terminal diagnosis. He even went a bit green, reminded me of a hangover I got from tequila one time. I never drank it again.

He put up his hands in protest, quavering voice, said: 'Just give me a week.'

'No problem.'

And I shot him in the two knees. Fuck it was loud. Took me a minute to make sure I wasn't after making myself pure deaf. Made a mental note to buy a silencer. On the floor, there was pools of blood and Bell was rolling around and roaring. *Christ above, Christ above. My fuckin knees.* All that. Dorothy was still screaming outside, something about the cops.

I bent down, leaned into his ear. Dust floating in the passing sunlight, sang like slow motion, sound waves reassembling from the echo.

He moaned when he sensed me coming, reduced to the primal fear. I let the terror flow through him, the lens of certainty take focus.

'I'll be back in a week. Next time it'll be your hands. Then your ears. Then your tongue. And eventually I'll pour acid in your eyes. So do yourself a favour, Michael, and get the fuckin money!'

Dorothy was pale as a vampire on the way out. Phone cradled between her ear and shoulder in shock. I asked: 'Do you know where you are now?'

And I left.

Big notions

Freddie was at the pub the following night. I was on the door when he came over to talk. Stubble, black t-shirt.

He said: 'Bell paid up this mornin.'

'That's that sorted so.'

'Did you shoot him in the two knees?'

'I wanted to make a point.'

'You fuckin did that alright. Half the other pricks that owe me money are tryin to pay up now too.'

'Proper order. Anythin else you need, let me know.'

'Are you round tomorrow? I have a few things lined up.'

'Sound. Gimme a shout.'

Beat, he lit a smoke, like he wanted to say something else, the neurons in his mind forming a tone. The sky tuned in, the clouds stalled to hear. He exhaled some chemicals, said: 'I heard you brought Karena home the other night?'

'I did. Do you have a problem with that?'

'She's a tasty bit of stuff. Did ya know she used to be blonde?'

'No.'

'Fuckin dyed her hair, somethin to do with her actin career. Big notions if ya ask me. She's a fuckin barmaid at the end of the day.'

'What's your point?'

'Girls like her bring lads in drinking. No point having a pig serving pints.'

'No. I suppose not.'

'But I've a rule about staff sleepin together.'

'Why's that?'

'Girl like her. Everyone wants her and it causes shite. Tried her myself one night and she told me to fuck off. Seems like you're the only one she went for so far.'

'Not my fault you're all puck ugly.'

'I couldn't give a fuck. But what if some night a fella's in buyin big rounds and puttin chat on her and then you don't like it.'

'That won't be a problem.'

'You sure?'

'I'm sure. '

'Cos you killed half the country after what happened your last burd and that's the kind of publicity I don't want.'

I waited to see if he'd push it, but he didn't. Just said: 'See ya later, kid.'

Salvation for the past

The bouncing became a regular thing. Good money and more time with Karena. Some nights, on the door, the rain danced on the streets, others it was a shy summer, like a warm blanket around the city. After work, she'd have the keys to lock up and do the tills. The others did coke on the counter and usually went to a party. When they'd all be gone, it was just me and her with the place to ourselves. We'd drink what we wanted and put on the music. Let Gogol Bordello play loud, echo off the empty walls. We could smoke when the place closed and the nicotine clouds drifted through the tunes, soft and potent, like nostalgia. We cleaned the bar to a bright sheen, put up the chairs, and swept the floors. You can hear the rattle of the bottles in crates as we stocked the bar, the clatter of the bucket and mop across the tiles, the rapid churning of the till spitting out the receipts as we enjoyed the scene and let the spirits cruise through the stolen night.

After, we'd go back to her place. Crash downstairs on her black leather couch, surrounded by a collection of vinyl records and bookshelves full of Stanislavski, Chekov, Mamet. She was a fan of crime too. Paul Williams. Nicola Tallant. Ken Bruen. Mick Donnellan. Other nights we'd go upstairs and lie down and find the source through naked music.

Tonight, Karena lit a stick of incense and her room smelled like sweet weed and flowers at a funeral. She was sitting on the bed, against the headboard, dancing eyes, black jeans, white shirt, silver watch on her wrist. Her face had a glow in the dim lamplight, an aura I hadn't seen before, like a gambler after a big win. She was having a joint and we got talking. Her past, her family, her ideas about the future. She wanted to move to London where it was better for actors. Especially women. And she loved the stage. It challenged her the most but didn't pay enough.

She liked roles with strong female characters. It was important that women had an artistic voice. Ireland was a male dominated country in everything. Politics, business, the arts. Called herself a method actor, which means she lives the part. Takes on the personality, mannerisms and emotions of the character. She called it *empathy*. Living another life, getting drained by a phantom organism, a creative doppelganger dictating her day. Her decisions. Her words. People don't recognise her when she's in this zone. She compared it to Natalie Portman's rigorous training in ballet for *Black Swan*. Or Charlize Theron playing a serial killer in *Monster*. Daniel Day-Lewis going to jail for his part in *The Boxer*. Cillian Murphy's haunting role in *Oppenheimer* and his transformation in *Breakfast on Pluto*. It's her favourite thing about acting but scares her when she has to do something tragic. Like be terminally sick, violent, or die. Like Cate Blanchett playing *Veronica Guerin.*

Screen acting was better money but last time she did a film the director stuck his hand between her legs in the taxi home. She told him to fuck off and hasn't been hired since – until now. The new film was haunting her. The closer she got, the less she could tell the two worlds apart. Where *she* ended, and her *role* began. What she felt, and what the character felt. Was she having her thoughts, or the character's thoughts? And when it ends, can she find a way back? She was so immersed in the universe of the script, like an emotional labyrinth, she worried if she'd be able to find her way home.

I asked her more about it. Who was she playing? Was it a real person? She said she couldn't talk about it. Not just because of the NDA now, but she was superstitious. The spell might break, and the other girl's spirit might get scared and abandon her and she wouldn't be able to do the job and her career would be fucked.

Two brothers. One married with kids. The other unmarried and gay and no kids. Her father teaches Irish at the university. Her mother is a librarian, recently recovered from breast cancer. Both expect her to get sense and become a teacher. One long term ex-boyfriend. A closet cross-dressing pharmacist who hated all things artistic – especially acting. Flings with theatre types. Girls and guys. One threesome. She prefers men but sometimes longs for the tender understanding of another girl's intimacy – especially her tongue and taste. And she likes control, to *fuck* rather than be *fucked*. A cousin in jail for attacking his wife. A big shock to them all. The idea of being related to someone *locked up*. She dried up here. The gods of conversation looked at me like it was my move, but I didn't bite. Then she hit me with: 'Were *you* ever in prison?'

'No. Why?'

She pushed her hair behind her ears, said: 'Cos I looked you up online.'

'And what did you find?'

She thought, searched for the word, said: 'A monster.'

'That's the internet for ya.'

'Some of it *must* be true.'

'Let them prove it.'

She was more curious than concerned, almost excited, said: 'So you never did time?'

She said *time* like she heard it on a film.

'Not yet anyway. I was in a reform school for a while. They're like jail for juveniles.'

'Sounds bleak. Where? What happened?'

'Sent down for robbing a bookie in Ballinrobe.'

She was confused, asked: 'What age were you?'

'Thirteen.'

'Where do you even start with robbing bookies at thirteen years old?'

'The tip came from one of the fellas working there. Lad called Eugene. He used to do the count every night, thousands and thousands, but he couldn't rob it himself. Too obvious.'

Incredulity, she asked: 'So he called in the local ruffians?'

'He always used his younger brother, Dave, for jobs like that. And Dave knew me and they needed someone else. It looked easy because the bookie kept his cash at home in a safe and Eugene had the code.'

'Why the hell would he have the code?'

'The bookie left it lying around where Eugene would see it. Then told him he'd be away for the night. Eugene was already under surveillance. They knew he was skimming an odd bit for himself from the count and were waitin to catch him. Eugene did the driving, me and Dave broke in, opened the safe, took the money back to the car and the cops surrounded us.'

'And you all got sent down?'

Sent down.

'Eugene went to Castlerea. Me and Dave ended up in St. Joseph's in Letterfrack.'

'What was that like?'

'Pure holiday. What do you think?'

'Was there...abuse?'

'Yeah, Dave had a tough time.'

'Not you?'

'They tried. It's where I learned all authority is corrupt, out to fuck you, one way or the other.'

'Did you stick up for Dave?'

'When I found out, yeah. A priest came in one night with

roaming hands, but I was ready. Stabbed him in the two eyes with a sharp pencil. They left us alone after that.'

Her head tilted in confused sympathy. 'Where were your parents?'

'Father died from a heart attack. Mother – suicide.' Then I said: 'It's too quiet here.'

She got up, went to the record player in the corner. Carpet floor, bare feet. Red painted nails. She looked through the vinyl collection. Asked: 'Fancy some Moody Blues?'

Nights in White Satin. Turntable, needle. Song. Taps into the ambience. Gathers up the room. Exorcised the fiddling priests and the cold walls of the institution. Everything got warmer, possible. Karena turned around, graceful beauty, took off her jeans, shimmering legs. She opened the skylight, lit another joint, exhaled into the dark, said: 'I'm tired now.'

'No more questions?'

'Tell me about El Niño.'

My mind swerved. 'Why?'

'It's part of you, and I want to know. I can feel your pain, and it shuts me out. It's like a wall between us.'

'Was there not enough about her online?'

'There was. But I want to hear it first-hand. From *you*. I remember her from college. She was stunning, and smart, and so charismatic and stylish. It was a huge shock when she died.'

'You *remember* her?'

'Everyone remembers her.'

'Did you know her?'

'No. We shared some English modules. I was mostly into drama and writing. But you couldn't forget her. We see millions of people every day but then we meet one like her and it's a new level of exotic luminosity. And she was like that, lit up the whole room, and after - everything went dark.'

Her eyes went murky and moist. I asked: 'Are you crying?'

'I'm sorry. I think I'm too stoned.'

'We might have enough talkin done.'

'I have. You haven't. Tell me about her. We can't just let her die out like that. We need to keep her alive, her memory, her life. Her hopes, her dreams.'

'The story ends in tragedy.'

'But this way we can save her. So it wasn't all for nothing.'

'By talking?'

'Beats drinking.'

She had me there.

'And it's a huge elephant in the Charlie room. About time we talked about it.'

'What do you want to know?'

'Everything.'

'That could take a while.'

'We have all night.'

'And it's *crimey* and sad.'

'Start with how you met her.'

Plate tectonics, a shift in my subconscious, her haunting resurrection, like she was in the room, conjured into consciousness. My heart broke with the first words, cracked by the weight of the guilty chains, dragging across the rusty floor.

'I stole her wallet.'

'And?'

'And then I called her up and asked her out.'

'Asshole. Keep going.'

Salty Blondes

Interior. Freddie's house. Afternoon. It was time to get paid. This is how we usually did it. Let a couple of weeks add up, then I collect a bundle. We were in the kitchen. He was in black combats and a Slipknot hoodie. Ginger stubble, smoking a rollie. There was a smell like stale milk and wet towels. He handed me the grade, said: 'Bit extra for the thing with the politician.'

I was sitting at the table on a rickety chair, said: 'Whatever's goin.'

'Just calm down on the thieving at the pub.'

'How do you mean?'

'I'm getting too many salty blondes asking to see the CCTV when their cash goes missing. Makes my ears bleed.'

I lit a smoke, didn't confirm or deny, asked: 'That it?'

'Anyone try to shoot you yet?'

'No.'

'McWard doesn't have the money anyway. I asked around.'

'The papers said there's other crews tryin to break in. Maybe that's keeping him busy. Probably somethin we should keep an eye on too.'

He took a long pull, wasn't sure if it hit, took another and sucked in deep, said: 'Let him be the lightning conductor. They'll start with him, then we'll know what we're dealin with.'

He let out a blast of smoke, twigged like he just thought of something, said: 'You livin with Karena now?'

'Nothin official. Could be there, could be on benches, the beach, the brothel. No fixed abode.'

He thought about it, said: 'You should go on the list for a council house. Like this place. Cost you fuck all, and you need to be showin an income in case the CAB cunts come after ya.'

'Who's the CAB cunts?'

'Criminal Assets Bureau. I'm only paying €30 a week here, but at least I'm in the system. I could buy a mansion for cash but then they'd be all over me like the fuckin monkeypox. Way it is now, I have a housing need, just like you. The pub and all that is not in my name so they can do fuck all about it.'

'€30 a week? Not bad.'

He got a text, read it, exhaled in anger, said: 'Fuckin ex has me robbed with maintenance for the young fella.'

'You've a young fella?'

'Yeah, Ryan. He's five now. Herself is a pure bitch though.'

'Could ye not get on?'

'She went mad after he was born. Tried to kill herself a few times. She's with some other prick now.'

'Do ya get to see him much?'

'Ryan? Yeah. I get him once a week. He's on the spectrum, loves goin on the train, pretending he's a conductor, collecting tickets. The other passengers love it, they all play along. I even got him a little uniform and hat and everythin.'

He showed me the picture. It was like a smiling mini-Freddie in a waistcoat with *Irish Rail* written on it.

'Cute as fuck, isn't he?'

He put the phone back in his pocket, said: 'There's a special needs payment for it too and herself gets that but she's still fuckin hauntin me for more. Anyway, the more I can screw the government, the better. I need to look like I'm poor, can't afford fuck all, so they can't come after me for tax and souped up child payments. You should try it. I get the TV licence as well. And medical card, fuel allowance, and I hurt my back a few years ago so I get a disability allowance for that. I'm waiting on my free units for the ESB but the bastards don't want to give it, tryin to *means test* me. Fuckin discrimination. I'm tellin ya. Last bill was nearly €150. Practically a week's dole. Good thing I'm gettin a magnet for the meter.'

'Magnet?'

He spun a circle with his finger, said: 'Magnets stop the yoke goin around. Keeps the cost down.'

'What yoke?'

'There's a spool inside the meter box. That's what puts up the units and it's the units that cost the money. If you stop the thing goin around, you don't get charged. Simple. There's a lad droppin fifty down from Tyrone next week.'

'Fifty magnets? For what?'

'We're goin to sell them.'

'To who?'

'You'll see when they land. But we have a different job before then. Are you here for a score on Saturday? Up your country, Ballinrobe.'

I got flashbacks, defensive, unsure, asked: 'What's *there* that's worth robbin?'

'You mean what's *not* there? Guards. They're closed most of the time now.'

'So?'

'So there's a handy ATM on the main street, wide open for the taking, could be €80k. What do you reckon?'

'Sounds better than the fuckin meter boxes.'

Molly Sweeney

Interior. Town Hall. Galway. Karena had a part in a play and she made me come and see it. I sat down the back with a naggin. Audience around me spoke in hushed tones and reverence for the cast – especially *her*. I found a programme on the floor. Opened it up. Freddie was right about the blonde hair. It was shorter in her headshot, just below her ears. Her blue eyes radiating from the page. Few lines about her too. Experienced. Qualified with an MA in Drama and Theatre studies at the University of Galway. Enjoyed critical acclaim in award-winning performances around the country. Writing prizes for short films and screenwriting competitions. Represented by all the top agents. Described by the Irish Times as a ".... revolutionary Irish talent, pioneering a new generation of transformative female artists and will certainly contribute to Ireland's position as a globally dominant force in all things theatre and film...."

So why the fuck is she working in The Galway Hooker?

The show began. She was playing a blind woman that regains her sight. Alongside an eccentric husband and a washed-up optician with a dying flair of genius. She stole the show. Stood under the spotlight and elevated the crowd to a new realm of theatrical appreciation. They were fixated, static, mesmerised and awed. An old woman cried. Life was brutal when it ended. The raw light, the cold draught from the door, the phones pulling focus, the sad empty stage and the lonely darkness.

Went to the bar upstairs. Bright lights. Wooden chairs with thin legs. The courthouse across the road. Had flashbacks of my time there. Dodged a long sentence, got sober. Became a student. Chance at a better life. Until...

Ordered a vodka. Drank it straight. Washed it down with a cider. Acting types standing around. Drinking spritzers. All raving about the performance, the talent, the famous people that were there.

Karena was backstage. Doing the "Get-Out" whatever the fuck that was. She sent her friend Stephen to tell me. He was thin, loose jeans, gay, soft spoken. I offered him a drink. He said he'd have a gin&tonic. Cheeky fucker.

We took seats. He opened with: 'Karena is amazing.'

He put real emphasis on the *azing* part.

'I know, thanks.'

'Are you sure you deserve her?'

'No, not at all. Why?'

'She's destined for much bigger things. What did you think of her performance?'

'Top class. It's my first time seeing her in anything.'

He pulled a face saved for homophobes, said: 'Seriously?'

'Not really my scene, Steve.'

'You should pay more attention to her career. Did you notice tonight how she *became* the character?'

'That's the empathy thing, the method stuff?'

'Do you know how hard that is it do? The rest of us *act,* but she goes to a different level. *She becomes.*'

'I know her mostly as a barmaid, that's why I haven't seen much.'

He huffed, crossed his legs, said: 'The Galway Hooker? She does that for the money but it's such a toxic hole. They don't hire LTGB people. It's like... so obvious. The guy that owns it definitely has issues.'

'I'll give him your feedback.'

'Don't bother.'

'Anyway, does this theatre shit not pay? There was a big crowd down there.'

'It all goes on the production costs. The real money is in the movies.'

'I think Karena's workin on one right now.'

He clammed up, said: 'She's not allowed talk about it.'

'Hard to take an interest in her career when it's top fuckin secret.'

'She's right. She can't jeopardize it by telling *a guy*. You could tell someone else, and they could steal the idea, or the tabloids could get it and the whole suspense would be ruined when it comes out. Not worth it.'

'Do you know what it's about?'

'No. Just anything she's part of is always *the best*. And it's a huge company behind it so she's going to be a star soon.'

'Talented lady.'

'We're going to miss her when she moves to Hollywood.'

She arrived then. Black jeans. Green jumper. Hair down. Headband. People kept stopping her to tell her she was great. She took it all demurely, gave them enough time to feel special, then excused herself and came over, gave Stephen a kiss, said: 'Hi, babes...'

'Love you girl.'

Then to me. 'We ready?'

Walking up Eglington Street. Dark, orange lamplight, cars splashing through puddles. Drunk students outside the Franciscan Monastery. Singing, laughing, taking pictures. She took my hand, said: 'Thanks for coming.'

She was surreal in the night, still glowing from the performance. I felt like I'd stolen her, as if she was something rare that belonged back in the museum of the Town Hall.

'You're more famous than ya told me.'

She shrugged, went: 'It's nice to be talked up, but I'm only as good as my last performance. Tonight's over now, that's it. I'm out of work until my next gig.'

'Is that why you have to keep up the bar job?'

'I like working there too. It has its perks. Like *you*.'

Walking by The Cellar, I said: 'I can fund your career if it helps?'

'I'm not a charity case.'

'But you can't waste your talent serving pints to rednecks.'

'You trying to be my sugar daddy?'

'No, but I have money and you don't. And you have talent, and I don't. There's an equation there somewhere.'

'I'd feel too guilty.'

'Why?'

Crossing the road in Eyre Square, she dodged the question, said: 'I should have the advance from the movie soon anyway. Once the shoot starts, all the fees come in. Did you enjoy the play?'

'I'd tell ya if I didn't.'

'I wanted you to understand what I do.'

'I kept the programme too. Why'd you change from blonde?'

She was shocked. Something changed. She let my hand go, became someone else, a stranger I never knew, the blonde version unmasked. She looked older, colder, foreign. I thought I was hallucinating with drink induced dementia. Even her voice went briefly off key. She covered her mouth, said: 'I forgot about that picture.'

She touched her hair. 'It's for the part, maybe I'll change it back after. I'm not sure. What time is it?'

Now she was *Karena* again. Composed, like the warm blood of life was flowing back through her. I said 'Ten.'

'Shit, my shift started at half nine.'

Fuzzy

McWard turned up at the pub. Him and the wasters from his flat. He was all pumped up and confident, like John Wayne coming into the saloon. The others had an alkaline smell, and a dead droopy look, like reluctant zombies.

He stood in front of me. Flabby stomach, shite runners, all cocky and said: 'Let us in.'

'We're finished.'

'Not for us, you're not.'

'For everyone. And you're not welcome anyway.'

'Why? Because you're afraid of me?'

'No, because you're dressed like a dirty dog and you smell like a stale box of onion rings.'

That took the air out of his balloon. I looked right into his eyes, big orbs of cowardice and hurt, knowing he'd never make a move, no matter how high he was. Some lads have it, and you know they have it, but not McWard. In a world of fight or flight, he always took flight. On top of that, Cally had flagged it with the lads inside and now there was another six bouncers behind me. McWard was no prophet, but he could see the damaged future.

He backed down, said: 'Keep it up, Charlie.'

And he fucked off.

The next night, he came back with a young girl. She was about fifteen. Pink short skirt, skinny, plastered in orange make-up. Pure tart. She was holding his arm to keep her balance.

McWard, brown boots and black jeans, went: 'Will you let me in now?'

'I already said you're not welcome.'

'This has to be discrimination.'

I pointed to the juicy fruit, said: 'And no minors after nine.'

She went for offended, like I'd farted in her face, said: 'Fuck you, asshole.'

'Her? Sure she's 21. Isn't that right, Chloe?'

'Totally.' She said.

'21 years of jailbait. You should be on the sex-offenders list. Now piss off.'

Chloe got indignant, asked: 'Why're you such a wanker?'

'I'm likin this, Charlie.' Said McWard.

'Likin what? Makin a dick of yourself?'

'All the excuses you're givin me.'

'You're not gettin in. So go and find a teenage disco for yourself and Chloe somewhere.'

She came back with: 'Why don't you find a personality?'

And she stormed off, her heels clicking and scraping, and McWard trying to catch up to her.

Karena and Cally came out for a smoke. She lit up a Carroll's, pulled hard, exhaled into the electric night. Large earrings. Shiny hair. She held the cigarette like royalty and asked: 'How's your night goin?'

'Alright, lotta gimps around.'

Cally looked towards the square, said: 'What the fuck is this?'

There was a motorbike coming, slowing down as it got closer. 'Looks like a Suzuki.'

'It's a one-way street.'

The driver reached inside his jacket and took out a gun.

He pointed it at me, but his hand wavered, like he was unsure. And he was losing control of the bike. He was trying to aim, and stay balanced at the same time, but the handlebars were going back and over, like a cow trying to shake off an attack of flies.

The first shot went through the window. A roar of breaking glass. People screaming inside. I pushed Karena to the ground. She was frozen, confused, her cigarette smouldering on the path.

Another shot hit the door, just above our heads. Splinters of wood rained down around us. Karena screamed: 'Christ! Charlie, what the fuck is going on?'

Cally pulled her inside and I got up to go for the shooter. He was off the bike and coming over. I knocked him onto the path and had him in a chokehold in seconds. He was light, weak and young. Kept pulling the trigger in a panic. Hitting anyone that might be in the way.

BANG! BANG! BANG!

A woman on the ground, shot in the stomach.

BANG! BANG! BANG!

A lifeless man on the road, blood all around his head.

I squeezed harder and got him unconscious.

The shooting stopped but people were crying, shouting into their phones for ambulances and guards. Sirens in the distance, survivors trying to do CPR and makeshift triage. The broken glass crunching under Cally's feet.

'Is Karena okay?'

'Yeah, she's inside. She wasn't hurt. Who's this fuckin eejit?'

I took off the helmet. Blonde hair. Starved, skeletal look.

Cally said: 'Fuzzy?'

'Fuzzy?'

'I know him. His name's Fuzzy. He's a hitman for hire.

Pure waster. Does jobs for McWard but always fucks it up.'

At least they weren't locals

The next day, sitting in Freddie's car, outside Rabbitte's on Forster Street. We were watching the crime squad going over the scene. They were in all the gear. White overalls, facemasks, forensic tools in a steel box for picking up the bullet casings. The Armed Response Unit was there too, making a show of force. Bullet proof vests, pacing back and over, guns ready.

I was smoking out the window, remembering the bike coming in slow motion, thinking I should have neutralised him sooner. Freddie was tapping the steering wheel, anxious, annoyed, biting his nails. He said: 'I knew McWard would come with somethin.'

'No, you didn't. You said he was broke and everyone thought he was a joke, and I had nothin to worry about.'

'Well, you're still alive, so I was almost right.'

'That must be why he was comin to the pub, watchin my schedule.'

'And he still managed to make a bollix of it.'

I pointed, said: 'Still, there was a couple down for the weekend that got killed.'

'At least they weren't locals.'

'What has that got to do with it?'

'Funerals would be a bitch. The city papers would get weeks out of it. At least now they can write about it up in Donegal or somewhere.'

Another squad car pulled up, two guards got out, young

and agile, started directing traffic, moving on anyone that stalled too long to stare. One of them noticed us, pulled out a pen and wrote something in his notebook. He looked over and Freddie gave him the finger.

'Got a letter from CAB too this mornin. Buncha fuckin haemorrhoids.'

'What they want?'

'Unexplained income. Gettin an audit from the revenue and the social have me cut off the rent allowance.'

'Fuck.'

'They checked out my ex and the payments for the young lad. Said I couldn't afford to give her what I was givin and still live myself. They know there's extra money comin from somewhere. They cut her off too. She's gone fuckin cracked. Denyin me access now and everything. All over *this* shit.'

'Can they nail you on anythin?'

'I don't know, I have a fella doin the books for me so I'll have to talk to him and come up with a story. I might have to pay them a bit to fuck off.'

'Cally says the shooter was a pure waster?'

'Fuzzy? Absolute reject. Couldn't shoot his load in a half-price whorehouse. He owes money to a few small dealers around. Got into the killin game. But he never killed anyone properly until now. At least nobody *right*.'

'What do you mean, *nobody right*?'

Freddie exhaled, like a man losing patience. 'He was supposed to do a Dublin fella in the Clybaun hotel but he shot the doorman instead.'

'So, he has shot doormen in the past?'

'Yeah, by accident though, so it doesn't really count. Then there was a lad in Bohermore that owed McWard money, and he fired shots in the letterbox.'

'And?'

'Wrong letterbox. Some granny got it in the knee.'

The guards were discussing something now, throwing more looks our way. Freddie continued. 'And I think there was somethin to do with a car chase in Salthill. He was on the way to do a job but he was braggin about it in the pub beforehand and an undercover cop heard him…. I don't know. Where is he anyway?'

Cut to: Salmon Weir Bridge. Night. The roar of the water. The Cathedral frowning in stern disapproval. Concrete blocks tied around Fuzzy's legs. The way he whimpered, like a bag of puppies.

'Where do you think?'

'Did he suffer?'

'No, Freddie. It was tranquil. And I'm goin to sort out McWard next.'

'How?'

'I'm goin to go to his apartment and give the coroner some overtime.'

'No point, I tried it myself this mornin. He's gone. Layin low. He knows you'll be out gunning for him now. His whole place is cleaned out.'

'Prick. I should have done him the first time I was there.'

'We'll get him. *We'll get him.* Be tranquil. We need to let the cops calm down too.'

'Do we not have a few of them on the take?'

'We do, but none of *these* fuckheads. They all think they're on *The Untouchables*. And the ones we *do know* aren't happy with the attention either so they're staying clear.'

One of the scrubs took a blood sample off the ground, examined it, and put it in his bag.

'What if he'd hurt Karena?'

'I'm not happy either, Charlie. Don't mistake my calm demeanour for a calm demeanour. Gimme a few days and he'll be found.'

'And what then?'

'Then no more tranquil.'

A bus behind us beeped because it couldn't get through. One of the cops came over, banged on the bonnet, shouted: 'C'mon, move!'

He was baby-faced but well built, like a hurler in his prime, competitive confidence of a team leader.

Freddie blew the horn, shouted: 'It's my pub, ya prick.'

He pointed at us, all strict, said: 'Go! Now.'

Freddie started the car, revved hard, aggressive, pulled away, opened the window and spat at his shoes, said: 'Fuck yourself.'

Coming around by Eyre Square, I lit another smoke, contemplated the restless time ahead, asked: 'Anythin lined up while we're closed?'

'Yeah, there's that job in Ballinrobe. And don't forget about the magnets.'

'Let's start with Ballinrobe.'

The Front Door

Later, I met Karena in The Front Door. It was early evening, and the place was busy. Guinness going, ice rattling.

We took seats at a ledge by the window. It was handy because I could see everyone coming in or out. Nothing dangerous so far, just a busker outside playing *Spancil Hill* on the tin whistle.

Karena was in blue jeans. Black leather jacket. Red heels. Drinking vodka and Coke. No ice.

I went to the counter. Lot of aftershave around, and lads at the bar on their own, drinking Guinness and scrolling through their phone. The music was steady trance, like a calm end to an average day. The round came. Hers first, then a pint of cider for me. Brought them back. Left them down. She looked up, tired, nervous. Blue eyeshadow, white top. Her lip quivered, her hand shook.

'Anyone gettin killed tonight?'

Brown bag, gold strap. Sparkling rings, rouge painted nails. A perfume like citrus and orange.

'The ones that deserve it are gone on the run.'

'Those poor tourists.'

'At least you're ok.'

'That's not the point though, is it?'

I felt like I was talking to Freddie, but the roles were reversed.

'Should I even ask why somebody wanted to kill you?'

'It's a long story but it wasn't supposed to come to this.'

'How come they didn't arrest the shooter, did he just disappear?'

I went for equivocal, said: 'Yeah.'

'But I saw you through the window, tackle him to the ground?'

'I dragged him up the street to beat some answers out of him but he woke up and ran way...'

She was doubtful, said: 'I've been getting sick all day. Every time I think about it. The blood, the screaming, the gunshots. What are you even involved in? And Freddie, and the pub, they're saying CAB is investigating him now?'

The door burst open. She jumped in fright. I went for the Glock, but it was just a rowdy stag group knocking chairs, shouting and singing.

'I'm a nervous wreck.' She said.

'It's me they're after, they don't even know you.'

'But I nearly get killed in the crossfire - why does that sound familiar?'

We went quiet as the barman collected glasses between us.

'I got my schedule for the film. It starts next week.'

'Congratulations.'

'But I can't do it under this type of stress and pressure.'

'Once you're out of the pub it won't matter, nobody even knows about us.'

'We can't know that for sure though, can we? Why don't you *stay* with me – like *move in*.'

'I thought you don't do housemates?'

'I'm terrified alone now. My whole sense of security is destroyed.'

'You're not afraid they'll look for me there?'

'That's exactly what I'm afraid of. And I'd like you to be *there* when they do.'

She stared at me, through me, beyond me, into my soul. 'I'm not trying to replace El Niño.'

'Me neither.'

'Then what's the problem?'

Ballinrobe

Interior. Range Rover. Three in the morning. I smoked through the open window, watched the sky. Stars shone, like eyes in the night, light wind through blades of grass in the black empty fields. We had a trailer attached, populated with a small digger. Wheels bouncing on the bumpy road, squealing their iron squeal. Freddie driving, Leonard Cohen on the radio singing *Joan of Arc*.

I turned to him and said: 'Explain it to me again.'

'We're going to steal an ATM. What some people call *Pass Machines*.'

'What're we goin to do with a *Pass Machine*?'

'Crack it open and keep the cash. We'll use the digger to get it out.'

'This reminds me of Oscar and his charity clothes bins.'

'Don't compare me to that fuckhead.'

'Have you done this before?'

'Yeah. Loads of times.'

'Really?'

'No. Never. Should be good craic, though.'

'That's what we're after, *craic* is it?'

'Well, we can't take a piss in Galway without some guard jumpin out of the toilet bowl, so we might as well expand our operations. And stealin ATM's is a big IRA thing so everyone will think it's them and leave us alone. The perfect crime.'

'What if they're not happy about it?'

'The Provos? They can file a complaint to the Bank Raid Regulator. Who gives a fuck if they don't know it's us? Here's the sign for Headford, is it far more?'

'Bout another twenty minutes.'

'The sign for Ballinrobe says to go right?'

'Yeah, but everyone knows it's shorter to go straight on.'

'Sound so.'

We went down through Glencorrib. Not a cop in sight.

Freddie said: 'Mad place growin up, this, was it?'

'Twas.'

'Yourself and Kramer cleaned it out?'

'Did most of the places around it.'

Hit Cross about ten minutes later. Went over the narrow bridge and made a clatter of noise as we hit a speed bump.

'Shocks must be gone.'

The air through the window was nitrogen cold. We drove on through The Neale. A one pub village. Next stop Ballinrobe. Aldi to the left. Slaughterhouse to the right. Bright streetlights ahead. We followed the road around for Main Street, clattering all the way, loud enough to be a Nazi army coming to invade. A light came on in a house above us.

I said: 'Look. Drive on, keep goin.'

'Fuck that. We're here now.'

'Someone is goin to have us clocked.'

'And what'll they do? Call the guards? Sure, we'll be long gone by the time they find us.'

The ATM blinked up ahead, beside the church, embedded in the wall of the Bank of Ireland.

'There she is. Winner, chicken dinner.'

We pulled in. Freddie threw me a balaclava, said: 'Here, throw that on.'

And we hopped out.

Exterior. Ballinrobe. Night. Hometown. Old town. Another town to rob town. There was a sense of social vacuum. Shops closed. Pubs closed. The grey hand of the government had picked the place clean. The icy wind of progress like terminal cryogenics for the soul.

The path outside the bank glistened, a shimmer on the walls, the blank aura of concrete commercialism. Shaking trees beside the church. Macabre branches like brittle bones.

Then we heard: 'What're ye at?'

There was a grey-haired man staring down at us, unhappy with the whole scene.

'Who are ye? What're ye doin?'

'IRA!' Said Freddie. Go back to bed and mind your business.'

'I'm calling the guards.'

We ran around the back of the Range Rover. Freddie hopped on to the digger. It started with an angry growl. He reversed it on to the road and drove it towards the ATM. There was a high kerb, and it took three attempts to mount the path and get the angle right. The arm was like a demented maestro going up and down and sideways. He got it under control and aimed the bucket roughly where we wanted it and pulled the trigger.

There was a sound like crunching rocks and scraping metal. The gears kept grinding and catching and there was a smell like burnt copper and half-built houses. Reminded me of a dead dog my father buried in an empty cement bag one time. It took four swipes before the machine came loose. The screen went blank and there was wires and sparks coming from behind it.

More house lights came on, curious at the commotion. I

was getting nervous. Thinking there could be an attack from a local mob. Your man put his head out again, said: 'Go home ye dirty bastards, leave the bank the way it is.'

I picked up a brick and threw it at him. He saw it coming and ducked. There was a satisfying sound of breaking glass. Then he popped up again and shouted: "I'll fuckin kill ye!" And ran back inside. No doubt to get the gun he kept lying around. You could hear his wife screaming in the background. 'Leave it, Paddy. Leave it. Just let them go and they'll be gone!'

'I will not let them go!'

The ATM came loose and toppled onto the road. I ran over and helped Freddie load it. It was fierce heavy. Took an awful heave.

'Fuckin thing.'

'Must be full of money.'

'Hang on we nearly have it.'

It fell into the bucket with a disgruntled *thunk.* After, we used the digger to lift it on to the trailer. That's when we heard the first shot. It cracked one of the wing mirrors.

'What was that?'

Freddie was holding the side of his face. The shrapnel had grazed his jaw. 'Fuckin Lee Harvey Oswald. Hang on, I've a Magnum in the glovebox.'

'What do you want a Magnum for?'

Another loud blast shattered the wingmirror completely.

'Is it not obvious?'

He found the gun and fired towards the house. There was a deafening echo on the street. Then there was silence. We jumped in and sped away. I thought your man might be dead, but then the back window smashed as we took the corner into Church Lane. Fucker wasn't giving up. We got out of Ballinrobe but had to take the backroads to avoid the guards and it was freezing the whole way home.

Back at the house, we used drills to open it up and a load of cash fell out.

Took a while to do the count but we made €90,000.

€45,000 each. Not bad for ten minutes with a digger.

The next day there was talk on the news about an IRA raid on a bank in Ballinrobe.

The pricks didn't even deny it.

Locked Out

Still no sign of McWard. There was talk of him being gone to America, but I didn't buy it. Freddie said to keep a low profile after the shooting and he'd have lads out looking for him. It couldn't be that hard. Galway wasn't a big place and a fat bollox like McWard couldn't hide too easy. Few phone calls. Few house visits. I'd have him. I had big plans. Was savouring it. He was going to get it all. I warned Freddie to let me at him *first*.

Later, I moved into Karena's. She answered the door, hair in a ponytail, beige combats, red runners, asked: 'Where's all your stuff?'

'This is it. Me. I don't have anythin else.'

She exhaled in tired surprise, said: 'Come on in then.'

She spent the days filming, and we had the evenings together, mostly in bed. We'd let the calm take hold, surf the wave as the night crept in. The touch of cold from the open window and the silence as the kids in the distance stopped playing on the street. When it got dark she'd turn on the light and close the window. I'd watch her figure cross the bedroom floor, a svelte angelic swagger. She'd put on a long shirt, be naked besides, and go downstairs. When she'd open the door, she'd look back, ask if I wanted anything, and I'd be stunned by her exquisite features. The way her hair fell across her face had an elegant flair of design about it. The perfect splinter in her flawless appearance. One knee bent, fingers lightly on the wooden handle, her eyes watery and sea blue and bursting with energy and intellect. I'd tell her no and listen to the light patter of her feet on the stairs. The noises in the kitchen. The sound of a tin box taken down from the cupboard.

She always liked a joint at night. It was a ritual. She'd take out the papers, the tobacco, the rock of weed, and I'd get the scent coming up the stairs. She'd go outside and sit on the step and look into the darkness and think about something. I don't know what. But she had to think about it.

Tonight, I brought a bottle of red wine and joined her in the soft Galway air, full of inclement possibility. Her eyes shone in the starlight and her lips were full and silver from the reflected moon. There was a smell like daffodils and the ocean, and fresh laundry. Small notes sailed from the record player upstairs, lonely ghosts, knocking on the physical realm, unable to break through.

'How's the film goin?'

'Fantastic. Stressful. Incredible. Terrifying. I'm not sure I'll survive it.'

'Are ya doin your own stunts?'

'I don't mean like that. I won't be able to recover. I won't know who I am when it's done. I'll be locked out of myself.'

'Has that ever happened to you before?'

'I was never this involved in the story. I feel like I've taken it too far and the lines are blurred between the realities. What if I don't want to come back?'

'You didn't go blind after your last show in the town hall?'

'I didn't want to be blind. I spent days with my eyes covered. Cooking, eating, going to the bathroom, finding my way around the house. But when it was over, I was relieved. But this...I'm liking it too much. Maybe it's who I really am? What if life through art is real life, and the rest is just a simulation. Like we're all bored extras that don't really exist until the big moments. And then, on stage and screen, we come alive, and that's who we really are?'

'That would make everyone an actor waiting to perform.'

'But what if the audience experience it through us, and

that's why art is important. It makes everyone feel alive, and identify with who they're supposed to be, or not supposed to be? As actors we're like vessels for everybody's feelings, real life examples of their private selves and sometimes we get frozen into a particular role and can never escape? Or we just click into a fictional mind and become that person forever, making them real, turning art into life, and what if the person we're playing used to be real and had died, and we play them, and get trapped, is the dead person alive again? Does the actor die? Who's *who*? When you go so far down this road, what happens? And that's where I am right now. Am I dead or alive? Am I Karena or…?'

'Who?'

Tender breeze. Her elbow against mine. Her lips as she dragged on the joint, squinted her eyes. 'I'm sorry. What am I raving about?'

'No idea, kid.'

'Tell me some good news. Did they find that McWard idiot?'

'No, he might have emigrated.'

'Further the better. I saw there was a body washed up in the river, I thought it might be him.'

'I would have heard if it was.'

'The make-up girl in my trailer said it's connected to the shooting at the pub. If it's not McWard maybe it was the guy that pulled the trigger? The one on the bike? We never found out where he went. Did we?'

Fuzzy.

Didn't tie them blocks tight enough.

Fuck.

'I guess we know now. Fella like that probably had a lot of enemies.'

'Like you and Freddie?'

'And others. I heard he killed a doorman in the Clybaun hotel. That might have something to do with it.'

She wasn't convinced, asked: 'Why is there a shoebox full of money under the bed?'

'That's my shoebox full of money.'
'Have you never heard of a bank?'
'I robbed one the other night. You want me to put it all back in?'
'How can you rob a bank at night?'
'It was an ATM raid.'
'That was you? In Ballinrobe? I saw it on the news. You're goin to end up in jail, I know it.'
'I'll talk to Freddie about puttin the cash somewhere.'
'Just get it out of here. If you're goin to be doin that kind of work there'll be cops. And if there's cops they'll find it. And if they find it they'll ask me how the hell I didn't know it was there.'
'It'll be gone tomorrow.'
'You can leave some to keep me goin if you like.'
'How's two grand?'
'It'll help with the bills.'
'What bills?'
'We have to film some scenes in London and Berlin as part of the funding contract.'
'Beats Galway.'
'And the gang war.'
'How long is the shoot anyway?'
'Three months. And we'll need to do some screenings and PR abroad before bringing it here.'
'Why?'
'Because Ireland doesn't respect homegrown talent until it succeeds internationally...then they roll out the red carpet.'
'Do you have to ride anyone on screen?'
'One of the hottest guys on the planet. Would you have a problem with that?'
'Not my ideal night at the cinema.'
'I'll just pretend he's you.'
'I'm not sure that helps at all.'
She got sad then, with: 'What are we going to do?'
'When you leave?'

'Yes, if this takes off. I could be gone forever. I think that's what's really screwing me up. The conflict between this life and the other. Falling for you here, dragged away there.'

'You'd be crazy to stay around here. Imagine your audience watchin this scene now. Someone like you, here with someone like me. They'd think: what the fuck is wrong with her? She should hit the road the first chance she gets.'

'And that wouldn't upset you at all?'

This was déjà vu. A scene from another life, another universe. I said nothing. Lit a smoke, felt old, like age was teaching me something. Wisdom I was too drunk to understand. She stood up, said: 'See you upstairs.'

The Accountant

I rang Freddie, asked him what he does with his cash.

'You'll need to talk to my accountant.'

'Who's that?'

'I'll send you the address and tell him you're on the way over.'

'What about the CAB investigation?'

'He has that sorted, don't worry. Another thing, I've a job in Roscommon. Debt collection again, how're ya fixed?'

'Sign me up.'

The accountant had a place in Oranmore. Beside a salon. Up a stairs. Stern bitch behind a counter. Blonde, too much make-up, general hatred of men.

Name on her tag said: Attracta.

Told her I was looking for Ultan.

She went for surprise, with: 'Ultan?'

'Yeah.'

'Why?'

'Freddie told him I was comin.'

Her face changed. A *more of this* look. She picked up the phone. Spoke. Left it down, then told me to go through.

His office had a grey carpet. A large desk. A computer, and Ultan in a suit. Black jacket. Yellow shirt. Navy tie. Young. He stood up, nervous, said: 'Charlie?'

'That's me.'

'You're workin with Freddie?'

'I am.'

'And you want to?'

'Did he not explain?'

'He did. How much are you looking to wash?'

'I have €40,000 in shoeboxes.'

He frowned, asked: 'That all?'

'Is it not enough?'

'No. Just. I thought…'

'Don't think, Ultan. Can you do it or not?'

'Of course.'

'How?'

'I'll put it through the pub and security firm. It'll appear as wages in your account and payment for contract work. I can do the tax on this end. Do you have a bank account?'

'No. Never had. Don't believe in them.'

'You should really get one. We can use the company account for now. I'll issue you with a debit card and you can spend on that.'

'What's your fee?'

'5%.'

'And you won't screw me?'

'No.'

'Won't disappear with the money?'

'I know better than that.'

'What about the Criminal Assets Bureau? Freddie said you have them sorted?'

He stuttered, said: 'I'm dealing with it. They don't have a case, trust me.'

Beat, I thought about the angles, said: 'What if I need to take it all out someday?'

'Just gimme some notice. 24 hours should be fine. Do we have a deal?'

I left the boxes on the desk. He frowned at them, like he was wondering if the money would smell like feet. 'We'll start with this and see how it goes.'

'Ok.'

'Who else do you work for?'

'Excuse me?'

'What other gangs?'

'Nobody. Except Freddie.'

'Good. Keep it that way. I don't want a conflict of interest.'

'You don't need to worry.'

'I don't. You do. Fuck me around and I'll open your head.'

He swallowed, went pale, said: 'Of course.'

And I walked out.

Attracta was still behind the desk, ready to piss vinegar.

Bye now, I said. Thanks.

Tommy Ryan

His name was Tommy Ryan. Owned a petrol station in Roscommon. Fell into 250k debt in the Four Aces and disappeared. Freddie asked me to drive up and see if I could find him. He gave me a Ford Focus for the job. Got it off a woman that couldn't pay her loan. Nice wagon, well kept, sturdy. I found a Paul McCartney CD in the glovebox. Stuck it on and went up the N17, listening to music and smoking out the window. Got hooked on *Egypt Station.* Had a strong flavour of *Strawberry Fields* and dead Lennon.

Got to Roscommon town. Through a roundabout. Up a street with cafes and pubs and a bank. Parked outside a hotel with a coffeeshop attached. Could see Tommy's place up ahead.

Got out. Lit a smoke and let the cold breeze blow. It had a bite today, a threat of severity if you weren't careful. Zipped up the jacket and walked. Exhaled the Benson and let the pain in my windpipe pass. A scream against chemicals and carcinogens.

Walking was dodgy. Degeneration Cerebellum. Felt a bit shaky too. Somewhere, a room full of demons were bursting to escape. I'd have to keep them locked in with a blast of something strong. Might get this wrapped up fast. Back in Galway for a long evening of dark drunken anaesthetic.

The place was quiet when I walked in. Typical shop, deli, gravy, salt, Tayto, the usual. One old fella buying a stew dinner. He smelled like manure and cow's urine. A brown haired young one behind the counter, scanning pictures on her phone. Name on her tag said: ***Maggie.***

Asked her: 'Tommy around?'

She looked up, then back at the screen, and said: 'Tommy?'

'Yeah. Tommy.'

'He's not here at the moment.'

'When's he back?'

'I don't know, he's *supposed* to be here this evening.'

She looked up again, tried to figure out who or what I was. Then she decided she didn't care and asked: 'Do you have a card or something?'

Left again. Stood in the forecourt. A light drizzle started. Not much else happening, just time coming in for the kill. Spotted a pub across the road. The Swinging Lantern.

That'll do.

Got there. An alcove, then a door. Old signs for Harp and a smell like ale and red lemonade. Inside, the cushions were torn on the stools. Oul lads at the bar, staring at pints. A line of taps along the counter. A host of spirits on the wall. It was almost perfect but the young lad behind the counter was useless.

I asked for a Heineken and the keg went. The tap spluttered and spat white innocent suds into the glass. He didn't know what was wrong, so I ordered a Jim Beam and explained. He went to change it. I drank the Jimmy in two seconds flat. It put things into focus, sharpened the pixels, toned down the existential noise. There was a clatter of barrels banging somewhere out the back. Then he returned. Pulled the tap down uncertainly. It spluttered a bit more and went into full flow and I eventually got a pint of Heineken with a huge head, coming over the glass like a baker's hat. I let it slide, drank deep. Three pints later, I spotted *The Sunday World* in the corner beside an ancient Trocaire box. Opened it up. They had a picture of the couple that was killed last week and a shot of the pub's broken windows. My recent history was mentioned too. Detective Malone still dead and Charlie the chief suspect released without charge due to a lack of evidence. I read some more. They had a whole section on gangland. Talked about the power vacuum since Kramer's exit. It was all a bit of a thriller. A sense of: what next? They had pictures of McWard and another prick sticking their fingers up at the camera. A scene from a court case years ago. They'd gotten off too. Intimidated the witnesses into retraction. The cops looked annoyed behind them, pushing them ahead. The media giving them all the coverage they wanted. Real rock stars. They had a shot of me in a brown leather jacket holding a bottle of vodka. Standing outside Lydon Court with Kramer. Waiting for something, someone. Who knows? I had no recollection.

Everyone had a sobriquet because we might sue for defamation if they mentioned us by name. Freddie was "Frenchie" because they reckoned he could speak French. First I fucking heard of it. McWard was *Baby Sham* because his father was from Tuam and was always known as *The Sham*. They still called me Charlie because I was common knowledge by now. El Niño got a mention towards the end. The image hit me hard. Her brown eyes, black hair. Described as a young woman. Life cut short. Innocent victim. All that. I closed the paper then.

The pub was getting busy. People back from a funeral. Lot of ginger ale and hot whiskys going around. One or two asking for tea. There was a girl working now. Her name was Magda. Thin, Polish, dark eyes, tight hair. Severe efficiency, like her bones were frozen solid from the Warsaw winters.

I looked up when I heard her say: 'Thanks, Tommy.'

Tommy was bald and gaunt. Jaundiced eyes. A scarf and thin cheekbones. He sensed me looking, caught my eye. I looked back at my drink, knowing something telepathic had happened. He was eager to get out, pulled the door back and got to his car and took off. I watched him calmly out the window. Lexus, brand new, wine colour. I let him go, ordered another pint. Magda got it and said: '€4.50 thanks.'

I took my change, asked her: 'Was that Tommy Ryan gone out the door?'

'Yes, he's not looking too bad, thank God.'

'Was he sick?'

'He still is. Cancer.'

'I didn't know. I should call up to him. Is he still livin in the same place?'

'Meadow Court? Yes, he is. Nice houses.'

Meadow Court.

Brand new Lexus.

Handy enough.

Diary of a bad year

Exterior. Meadow Court. Evening. The door was open. Long hallway, leading to a dark kitchen. A stale smell, like wet clothes or mould. Noise to the right. Looked over. A living room. Fish tank, no fish. Big telly. Coffee table.

Tommy was sitting on a chair in the corner. Legs crossed. The chemo had him thin. Frail, emaciated. Reminded me of films I saw about Chernobyl.

The bookshelf behind him had history, travel guides, fiction. Tommy was reading J.M. Coetzee's *Diary of a Bad Year*.

Figure that.

'What's the story, Tommy?'

He stopped reading, said: 'You're Charlie.'

His voice was hoarse, weak.

'I am.'

'I knew it was you.'

'From the papers?'

'And the fact that you robbed my petrol station in Galway.'

'The Topaz?'

'Yes. I saw you on the TV, and then read about you in the tabloids, and knew it had to be the same notorious hero.'

'It was a complicated night.'

'It was my most successful shop. Then it closed, and I got into debt, and fell into gambling, and here you are again.'

'If not me, it'll be someone else.'

He left the book down. Seemed resigned, ready to give up. 'I worked hard my whole life.'

'And then you blew it all on a card game.'

'The game was fixed.'

'You shouldn't have been playing if you couldn't afford to lose.'

He looked around, like he didn't recognise the place, said: 'My wife left a week ago. She took the kids. Even though I don't have much time left.'

'She was right to take them out of danger.'

He coughed, rattled, wheezed. Pulled himself together and said: 'Are you going to hurt me?'

'Absolutely.'

'What if I had a proposition for you?'

'Is it worth a quarter of a million?'

'I own five more stations.'

'Why not sell one and pay us?'

'The banks have a hold on them, but you might know some people.'

'Like who?'

'The type that might want to offload some green diesel. We could pump it through the tanks.'

'What'll you charge for that?'

'Run it by Freddie – see if he'll take it off the debt. We could all do well out of it.'

'You won't be doin well out of anythin until you're clear with us.'

'I understand that.'

'So you have six stations altogether?'

'Five in operation at the moment. I can't get insurance on

the other one since you robbed it. Did you know Sharon, the girl you attacked, has brain damage and will never be the same?'

'I never got to visit.'

'And Trevor will be eating from a straw for months. And he needed surgery to wire his jaw back together.'

'Collateral damage.'

'I saw the CCTV. They didn't resist at all.'

'Good job or they'd be dead.'

He let that sink in, stared at me with his big eyes. 'You're empty, aren't you? Hollow, dead inside.'

'And I'm also in Roscommon and want to get home. What can you give me tonight?'

'I just played my best hand with the laundered fuel. Don't you think it could work?'

'I think you're a degenerate that would say anything to survive.'

'That's true. But you're interested?'

'I'll still have to break your arm.'

'How about I give you the Lexus instead?'

'I'll do both. It's important to make a point.'

Later, driving home, the Lexus was quiet. I had the window down, listening to the purr of the road going by, the air falling light on my face. There was a smell of silage and rain and it was getting dark, but not there yet, just a red glow haunting the twilight. Got to Galway and parked on the prom. Bought a bottle of red wine and drank it on the beach. After, felt heavy and tired. Walked up to Devon Park. Went left at Dr. Mannix Road. That scent of weed as I walked in the door. Went up the stairs and into Karena. She was asleep and there was call sheets and bits of scripts left around. Lied down and smelled her hair and let my mind roll, the normality of it. The possible. She backed in against me and got comfortable. I closed my eyes and heard

Tommy scream, the crack of his bones, the sad Roscommon sun watching the scene. Dead inside, hollow, empty.

Ballybane

Interior. Karena's room. Morning. Bright solar rays bouncing off the bedsheets. My phone rang, like Satan's bell. It was Freddie. He said: 'The magnets are here, are ya right?'

'Yeah. Twenty minutes.'

'Meet me in Ballybane.'

Karena was downstairs. Sitting at the kitchen table. Working on her laptop. It was the first time I saw her wearing glasses. Red frames against the blue glare of the screen. She was on a video call. A guy talking about film stuff. He was young, soft skin, American accent, impossibly good-looking. Figured it was the co-star. Mr. Love Scenes. He went quiet when he saw me, got nervous, like I was the grim reaper. That's the way to have him. In case the cunt got notions.

Karena turned around in fright. Pushed the screen closed, said: 'Hi…'

'I have to meet Freddie.'

'Ok, sorry, just discussing work.'

'Your eyes are all bloodshot.'

She frowned, said: 'I know, it's the irritation from my contacts.'

'You wear contacts?'

'Just for work. Did you get rid of the money upstairs?'

'Yeah, Freddie knows a guy.'

'Is he putting it through the pub?'

'I don't know, why? It's a guy in Oranmore. It's all gone

except for what I left you.'

She smiled, said: 'Thanks. Where are you goin?'

'Ballybane. Selling magnets.'

'Magnets?'

'Don't fuckin ask.'

There. It was cold, quiet, grey. Freddie asked: 'What's the story with the Lexus?'

'Down payment from Tommy Ryan.'

'Where's the Ford?'

'I told him to keep it.'

'Good swap. How's he fixed besides?'

I explained the diesel plan and he said: 'Could work, but we'd have to deal with them fuckers in the North and they can be tricky.'

He held up a big brown box of small coin shaped objects.

'Anyway, that's them.'

I took one out. They were heavier than they looked. Like a fat €2 coin.

'How much for one?'

'€50.'

'Bit steep?'

'They'll be savin it on their bills.'

I threw it back, said: 'It's too amateur, I don't get it.'

'It's not about the magnets or the money. It's about stayin in with the locals, keepin them on side. Letting people know we're still in business, pullin strokes, sayin *fuck you* to the gangsters in government.'

'Will it make us rich?'

'Only in social capital, Charlie. And that's priceless.'

We drove into the estate. Bins and bikes and burnt-out

cars scattered around. Houses with boarded up doors and metal frames on the windows.

'Is there nobody livin in them, or what's the story?'

'Council.'

'How d'ya mean?'

'They have to be up to EU standard. But the council won't spend the money to do it. So they're left empty. See what I mean? Government doesn't give a fuck.'

We got out. Lit smokes, let the noon air say hello.

A fella walked up in a leather jacket and last year's shirt. Bad teeth and cheap jeans. Asked us: 'What have ye?'

'Magnets.'

'The ones for the *ESB*? I was lookin for them.'

'How many do you want?'

'I've four brothers.'

'So five altogether?'

'No. Four. One fella is too honest.'

'God love him. We'll give you four for €150.'

'Can I pay you Friday?'

'You can fuck off.'

'I'll give you €50 now, so.'

'And I'll give you *one* magnet.'

'Deal so. And I'll get the rest Friday if it's any good.'

He took out a €50 note, handed it over. Freddie took a look, tore it in two, threw it on the dirty path.

Your man said: 'Hey, what're ya doin?'

'We don't take fakes.'

'That's *real* money.'

'You might as well be photocopying your arse.'

He bent down to pick up the swirling dud, said: 'Shower of wanks.'

We walked around the corner. Saw an open door. Knocked.

A raspy voice from inside, said: 'Come in.'

Interior. Living Room. A man in a wheelchair and pyjamas. Moustache and smoking a rolled-up cigarette. Watching the telly but not really watching it.

I stood in the hall, let Freddie do the work. There was a liquorice smell of strong medicine mixed with toast. Saw the jacks, went for a fast piss. Old razor on the sink, one toothbrush. Green enamel. A tiny, frosted window. Torn slippers and an analogue weighing scale. Flushed and went back out. Freddie was showing him the magnets, explaining how they work.

After, he said: 'What would I want one of them for?'

'It'll save you dosh.'

'Sure, why would I want to save anythin at this stage?'

'Have you no medical bills?'

'Too late for that, lad. They kept me on the waiting list too long. Sure I'm fucked. Go down to Mary in 66. She'll probably want one.'

'Does she like a good deal?'

'She'll take whatever's goin. Tell her Jerry sent ye.'

Mary was a young mother with three kids. Torn blue jeans and a black Coat. Greasy hair and most of her teeth were missing so she talked with a lisp.

She asked Freddie: 'And how much will I save?'

'Depends on how long you put it on the meter for.'

'Will I just leave it on the whole time?'

'No, they'll cop on then you see. How much are they chargin ya?'

'I owe them €1200.'

'How come?'

'I don't know, arrears or somethin, that's just what they said to me. And they threatened to cut me off.'

'Ok, put this on every evening after six. Take it off first thing in the morning in case they come to investigate. And don't answer the door to anyone.'

'Sure I answered the door to ye?'

'We're alright. Be careful of the lads in the suits.'

She took one, held it up, said: 'My cousin Sharon got caught last year with one of these.'

'How?'

'The kids let your man in and he seen it stuck to the side of the box.'

'That's what I'm talking about. €50 so?'

She looked us up and down, said: 'Can I pay ye another way?'

Freddie looked at me, said: 'Have you anythin to do for half an hour?'

I sat on the wall outside. Loving the social capital. Listened to the noise of life, people arguing, loud televisions, kids screaming, cars revving, radios playing dance music. Dogs barking.

Then I heard: 'My mam wants a magnet.'

He was a young teenager.

'Who's your mam?'

'She lives in 49. Jerry rang her and told her ye're around.'

I looked back at Mary's house, said: 'Freddie's just finishing a deal here. We'll be up then.'

'Don't go to 46 because the man that lives there is dead.'

'He probably won't want a magnet so.'

'Probably not. He hung himself with a dog chain. Depression, he had.'

'Sounds like it.'

'My mam said we can get money for killin you.'

'Hundred grand if you're interested.'

'Nah, thanks. She says you're good people. One of our own and to leave you alone.'

'Tell her I said thanks.'

He took out cigarettes, offered me one, I said no. They were the same packaging from the van I picked up in Loughrea.

He lit up, asked: 'Do you know McWard?'

'I met him.'

'He's a real fat bastard, isn't he?'

'He is.'

'My mam says he looks like a swelled pig. Do you sell drugs too?'

'No.'

'I'm thinking about leavin school.'

'To sell drugs?'

'Or pull strokes. I don't know which yet. Could I work for ye?'

'Ask Freddie when he comes.'

'I don't like him.'

'Why not?'

'My mam says he's two-faced.'

'In what way?'

'I don't know what she means. She doesn't like him anyway. I want to be more like *you*.'

'I doubt that. Is your father still around?'

'He's in jail.'

'What's he in for?'

'Robbin a post office. He got ten years. I was five when he left. He'll be out soon.'

'What then?'

'Me and him are goin fishing. Do you like fishin?'

'No.'

'Will you give me a magnet for free? We've no money.'

'I can do one for half.'

'How much is half?'

'€25.'

'I'll give you €10.'

'€15 and then you leave me alone.'

'Ah feck it, you're grand.'

Beat, then I said: 'Here, fuck it. Have it.'

His eyes lit up. 'Are you sure?'

'Yeah, you can get me again.'

He took it, said: 'Thanks, Charlie. If you ever need a hand pulling strokes, let me know.'

'I will.'

'I live in 49.'

'You were tellin me.'

'My name's Darren. Maybe I can help you find McWard.'

'How?'

'He's closer than ya think.'

'How close?'

'Look, here's the guards now. I better go.'

The squad rolled in. Sleek and quiet, crocodile style. There was a muted hum around the place. Tangible tension and disgust. They drove slowly. Circumvented an upturned pram. I kept my head down, looking at a stone on the ground. Then I heard the squeal of the brakes. The driver's door opened, and a young cop got out. I recognised him from the day outside the pub. Directing traffic. He had banged the bonnet and told us to go. He scanned around, tucked in his shirt, then reached back into the car and took out a baton and walked over.

'Charlie. Just the man. I have a present for you.'

'Is it Christmas already?'

'It's an arrest warrant. You're wanted at the station.'

'I thought you were more of a lollipop man?'

He loved that, said: 'In the car, c'mon.'

'Sounds like a waste of petrol. What have you got on me? Tabloid fantasies?'

'We've a lot more than that. It's about time we put you away.'

'That's what Malone thought too.'

He held up the baton, said: 'Don't bloody test me.'

'You're testin yourself, boss. You're in an estate, surrounded by my type of people, thinkin you can throw shapes. Do you want your car on blocks?'

That's when the first shout came. "Fuckin pigs!"

It was Darren. Holding a concrete block. He fired it at the car, broke the side window. It smashed in outrage and surprise. More shouts from everywhere. Abuse. Threats. Then they started throwing things. Bottles, cans, stones. The other guard got out, realized it was hopeless, shouted over: 'We better go, Joe.'

Joe turned around, trying to decide what to do. A rock almost hit him on the head. That's when he lost it and made a swing with the baton, caught me right on the nose. First, I saw stars, then felt the blood.

'Let's see what your supporters think of that. You scumbag prick. Now let's go.'

Mill Street Blues

Later in Mill Street Station. My face was numb, my nose fierce sore. It was hard to swallow, and I could still taste the blood. Joe had disappeared. Dealing with a woman guard now. Her name was Marion. We were in a box room. No air. No ashtray. She was intense. Energetic. Notions of promotion. Loved cases like mine. Good experience. Teaches her *the streets.*

She held up a biro, said: 'Let's start with the Topaz.'

'What's that?'

'We have a man of your build, with that same jacket you're wearing today, on CCTV doing the robbery.'

'It's a popular jacket. I'm an average height.'

Her tone was strict, like a nun in a school. 'Do all your lookalikes have friends called Oscar?'

'Who's Oscar?'

'He's the owner of a Toyota Starlet. Burned out in Barna. He told you he'd stolen it, didn't he?'

'Who'd want to steal a Toyota Starlet? Was he goin robbin a Novena?'

'We arrested him too. He's next door. Singing all about it.'

'What you arrest him for? Burnin his car?'

'He was caught him robbing charity clothes bins. And now we know who did the Topaz. Up in Ballinrobe lately?'

'Yeah, it's my hometown. That a crime too?'

'It is if you're stealing an ATM.'

'I heard that was the IRA.'

'They won't be happy with you spreadin rumours like that. Don't you know there's already a price on your head?'

'I did. Are you thinkin about it?'

'As much as I'd love to, someone has to be on the right side of the law.'

'There's a grave with my dead girlfriend down in Ballinrobe. Go down and take a look and tell me which is the better side then.'

'Always somebody else's fault. Typical narcissistic psycho. Her biggest mistake was ever having anything to do with you.'

'I'll admit to that. As for the rest, you need to charge me or let me go.'

'We can keep you for 24 hours for questioning. So get comfortable.'

Later, she was asking me more questions.

Why did you do the Topaz?

Why don't you confess?

Did I not care about Sharon? Or Trevor's broken jaw?

The customer paying for petrol was an American and this kind of thing gave the city a bad name.

And then there was Ballinrobe. The locals were terrified. Victimised. Afraid in their own homes. And where's all the money? No point lying, CAB are going to find it anyway. And what about all the people smoking the smuggled cigarettes? Did I not know they were full of rat poison? And what was I doing with a big box of magnets?

The door opened with a theatrical groan. A tall prick in a suit walked in. Long black coat, grey hair, holding a briefcase. He went for well scripted with: 'What's going on here?'

She looked up. Assessed him, seemed confused, asked: 'Are you in the right room?'

'This is my client.'

She pointed at me, said: 'Him?'

'Yes.'

'You're too expensive for *him*?'

'You need to leave now.'

'You should be ashamed of yourself.'

'And you should get out. I'm already thinking police brutality, illegal arrest, intimidation, no access to legal counsel. We're not in Nazi Germany the last time I looked.'

Marion got up reluctantly and left. Slammed the door on her way out. Just me and Armani. We stared at each other. None of us too sure how this was going to go. He opened with: 'I owe Freddie a favour.'

'You mean you owe him money?'

'That's between me and him. But let's just say I want my kneecaps kept intact after this, agreed?'

Beat. Then he said: 'You're agitated.'

'You'd be too.'

'Your file says you have a drinking problem. And now you're drinking again?'

'I need to detox from sobriety.'

'You know it can kill you?'

'The sooner the better. I'm too selfish for suicide.'

He sighed, looked at the ground. 'Doesn't matter anyway. If your health lasts, you have bigger problems.'

He took out a folder, opened it, said: 'Let's talk about the Topaz?'

'Nothin to do with me.'

'Who's this Oscar chap?'

'Never heard of him.'

'He seems to know you quite well.'

'Poor man is deluded.'

'Either way, he's causing you problems. We need to know his angle with all this.'

'Don't worry, I'll get on it. Can you get me out?'

'I can get you temporary release until your case comes up. Which will be soon. Unless the major witness has a sudden change of heart.'

'Happens all the time.'

Back at Freddie's, he said: 'Did they take all my magnets?'

'Whole fuckin lot of them.'

'Starved bastards. If Oscar can lead them to you, he can lead them to me, and the whole operation.'

'She said CAB are chasing the Ballinrobe money.'

'They can look up their hole. They'll find nothin. We're well covered.'

'So, what now?'

'We keep it simple with the bouncing and the lendin.'

'That solicitor said there'll be a case soon.'

'He said there *might* be.'

'How'll we get around it?'

'I'll leave that to your good self, Charlie boy.'

Amy

Exterior. Oscar's house. Night.

I came in the back door. He was cooking sausages in the kitchen. Turned in fright when he saw me. 'Charlie?'

'Things aren't good, Oscar.'

'I didn't tell them anythin. That solicitor got me out.'

'You didn't steal the car.'

'I couldn't. I don't even know *how*. I just wanted a few pound to help feed the kids.'

'How did they find out about the Topaz?'

'They told me they'd put the family into foster care, Charlie. I had to do somethin.'

'You're a rat, Oscar. You know the score.'

'No, I'm not. Wait. We can figure out a story, I'll tell them I was on drugs and didn't know what I was sayin.'

'It's too late for any of that.'

He hesitated, asked himself if I was serious, decided I was, then went for me. That's the jungle. Only one of us would be walking away. He was slow and foolish. Predictable. Easy to sort out. Used a steak knife I found beside the sink. Caught him around the neck. One deep cut from the jugular into the windpipe. He wheezed a bit then looked up at me with his innocent scared eyes. I felt paternal. A frequency from the far side of the future. A kid I might have had, or never live to see. Then he died and the cold smack of death filled the room. That's when I saw one of his kids standing there in her pyjamas. Amy, the girl trying to tune the telly the last time I was here. She was already crying. I lit a smoke and thought about what to do. Then said *fuck it* and left. A different kind of man would have killed her too, but she wasn't in the game, and Christ, you have to draw the line somewhere.

Serious escalation

Karena's face was warm in the morning. Her breath smelled of last night's cider. She held me tight as she slept, her legs wrapped around mine, her breathing in small heaves. I was staring at the ceiling, letting the waves come in and time do her dance. There was a heavy pressure in my chest and a piercing pain in my thumb, travelling up my arm. I tried to swallow but my mouth was too dry and my blood felt like rough sand labouring around my body. It was all a circulatory traffic jam, needing some oil, some gratified nerves to get things going. I got up without waking her. Her calm face, her deep sleep, her casual innocence.

Exterior. Galway. Day. Bright, like pain on the eyes. Arterial beats, like addicted urgency. Slow cars and calm pedestrians. The hum of lunch and life and normal routine. Spotted the Spar shop. Walked in. The news was on the radio. Serious concern at the rising crime rate in Galway. Another homicide last night. A traumatised child. A new low. A serious escalation. The drink was in a high shelf at the back. Wine, Prosecco, and beautiful Buckfast.

Opened it and took a long pull. The world swayed into a rearranged reality. Fella behind the counter gave me a quare look but said nothing. Paid him and got going.

Back outside. Here comes the focused rain. Those cracks in the cobbles, the scent of a passing girl's perfume. Chatter on phones, birds squeal and squawk, clouds darken, puddles glisten. A convoy of cops came from nowhere. Sirens going. A fire maybe, an emergency. But why the ARU? I walked over Cross Street. Followed the noise towards the docks. Went through

Druid Lane, through Merchant Road and Middle Street and around by Padraig's pub. Could see the lights as soon as I turned the corner.

Guards, forensics, fuckers with Uzis.

Ambulance with flashing lights and the ramp down.

A body on the ground. I knew the fat stomach before I saw the head.

McWard.

I rang Freddie, he said: 'Dead?'

'Yeah. Was it one of our lads?'

'All news to me, sham. Sounds like someone's making a move.'

'Who?'

'I don't know. But they reckoned the time is right to get rid of him. Where are you?'

'Still at the docks.'

'Meet me at my place and we'll make a plan.'

Spark the Baby Sham

It was all over the papers again. Journalists telling the story like they were writing a thriller. They had him painted as a *thug* and a *hoodlum*. A social disease in the local community. Direct descendant of Kramer and his vicious gang. A welcome relief to the guards that didn't have to be chasing him anymore.

Nothing about who killed him. There was hints of Westmeath, but nothing solid. He was such a dose, it could have been anyone. But why now?

'I thought you got lucky.' Said Freddie.

'No, I feel robbed.'

'At least it's burying the Oscar story. Wiped it clean off the news.'

I shrugged, admitted nothing, took another hit of Bucky.

'He was hiding out in them boarded up houses in Ballybane.'

'Where we sold the magnets?'

'Yeah, he was sneaking home at night for a shower.'

'Fucker. That young lad out there was tryin to tell me. Said McWard was closer than we think.'

'Who?'

'I think his name was *Darren*.'

'Oh him, yeah. Pure crayture. I tried to ride his mother one time. Couldn't get it up and she called me gay so I broke all her windows. Nice family besides.'

He opened a can of Budweiser, said: 'Anyway, I think we need to set up a commission.'

'What's that?'

'Lucky Luciano job. How they structured the mafia in the States.'

'We're not Italians, Freddie.'

'Are we not, Charlie? Fuck, that's that fucked so. Why do we have to be Italians?'

'I'm just sayin.'

'I want to gather up the bosses of the major gangs around the country and make rules, partnerships, deals. At least then, we'll know what's right and wrong.'

'And what if they say no?'

'Why would they say no?'

'What's in it for them when they can just come down and do what they want? Why would they suddenly sit down and start talking about partnerships?'

'Because McWard couldn't offer them what I have.'

'What's that?'

'I have all the contacts since I worked with Kramer. If they want to make a deal with anyone on the west coast, then I'm the only one that can swing it.'

'How's that work?'

'I'm talkin major quantity. McWard was living off old gear that was left over but nothin new was comin in. The smugglers didn't trust him. Or anyone else. But I can turn the key and get it flowin.'

'And what'll you get out of it?'

'Us, Charlie. *Us.* We're in a partnership now.'

'So, what'll we get out of it?'

'Security. Tax. Peace. I don't want people goin around

with a price on my head. That's alright for lads like you.'

'When?'

'I've a few rang. They're comin on Saturday. We have to go up to Athlone. Middle ground for everybody.'

'I don't see the point.'

'You wouldn't, but I have ambition. No offence.'

'None taken at all. What if they tell you to go fuck yourself?'

'They'll lose the contacts on the boats and they'll have to come back beggin me later.'

'Who did you invite?'

'Limerick, Sligo, Westmeath and one or two pricks from Dublin.'

'Do you want me there?'

'That'd help, Charlie, yeah, or are you busy ridin barmaids?'

'I might be busy ridin barmaids.'

'Or one of my whores. Did you ride any of them Turkish ones yet?'

'No, why?'

'One of them has AIDS, I'm not sure which. It's kinda like Russian Roulette with your knob.'

The Golden Rule

I was on the bed watching Karena get ready. Blue jeans. Black lace top. Brushing her hair. Things were good, McWard was gone, she wanted to go out for the day and live free, enjoy herself. It had weighed on her mind more than I knew or stayed sober long enough to realise. But now we could talk, arrange a future, make a plan, a way forward.

Then my phone rang. Freddie. I went downstairs. He said: 'What's the story with Oscar's child?'

'Which one?'

'The one that saw her father's throat cut?'

'Is she talkin?'

'Singin.'

'Fuck.'

'She should've been done too.'

'She's twelve years old.'

'Or thirty years in jail. Depends on how you look at it.'

'Can we get to the mother?'

'She's in rehab somewhere. All the kids are gone into Witness Protection. Where are you now?'

'With Karena at her place. How'll we play it?'

'I'd suggest you get the fuck out of Galway for now.'

'And go where?'

'Athlone. We have the meetin up there anyway. After that, don't come back until I can sort somethin.'

'Dirty fuckin cops pressuring a child.'

'It's your own fault. You forgot the golden rule.'

'What fuckin rule?'

'Don't go to bed with an itchy arse or you'll wake up with smelly fingers.'

Sewer dogs

On the couch. Waiting for Freddie. Window to the right, sun shining lightly, lightly shining, letting the day breathe. Karena had a scent like sweet sweat and moisturiser. Those red heels again. She was lying against me, feet over the edge, looking at the road outside. We weren't saying anything, like it was a painting, a frozen moment, our minds looking over millennia of time and emotion.

She had the fire going and there was a smell like cinnamon and burning timber. The mantelpiece had pictures of her in a red dress, shiny jewellery, impossible smile. Pizza boxes on the coffee table, left over from last night, beside a half-finished bottle of wine. Half-finished? I'd sort that soon.

'Is he on the way?'

'Yeah.'

'What did you do that's so bad?'

'Nothin. Just the guards are lookin for me.'

'They're *always* lookin for you.'

'They're really lookin for me now.'

'It must be somethin a bit *more* this time.'

Beat. Then she asked: 'When will I see you again?'

'I need a while up there.'

'How long?'

'A few weeks. Months. I don't know.'

'I can't come?'

'What about your work?'

'I could at least visit?'

'I don't want you connected to this.'

'You mean you don't want me to know what it is?'

'It's better you don't.'

'I'm sure I can handle it.'

'I don't think so.'

'It's not like I don't know enough already. I'm in this with my eyes open.'

'But this is different.'

'How?'

'Delicate. It needs time to simmer down. The less anyone knows about it the better.'

'Is it drugs?'

'No.'

'Those mysterious magnets?'

'Fuckin magnets.'

'Is it like *Goodfellas* when they robbed the bank but it's all going wrong?'

I got an image of Oscar's kitchen, the raw light from the dirty bulbs. Amy's pale face. The blood on the floor.

'No.'

'So, I'll just sit around? Waiting for you to show up?'

Pause, then: 'Ok, now I feel like we're about to break up.'

'Will ya fuckin stop?'

'I have that sick dread you get before someone tells you they cheated.'

'Cheated with who?'

'Some whore somewhere. Is that it? And she died, and you're covering it up like a serial killer. And Freddie's on the way over to smuggle you out of town?'

'Save that shit for your screenplay.'

'But there's something else on your mind. I can hear your thoughts rumbling and clattering, like a cranky engine. What is it, what happened? It's like you're in a room, with big thick walls, and I can't get in. Tell me the truth.'

'That's it. The truth. They're lookin for me.'

'They're lookin for you. *They're lookin for you.* Man of fuckin mystery.'

'What else do you want me to say?'

'Act like you give a fuck.'

'I do give a fuck.'

She sat up and stared at me. Hurt, angry. 'You give a fuck? Like fuck, you give a fuck. You don't give a flying fuck about anyone but yourself.'

She read my eyes, my expression. Looking for an empathetic direction. 'You're gone. You've crossed a line, the part of you that was human is dead. I don't feel our electricity, our chemistry, who are you now? You *did* kill someone, didn't you? And it's bad...'

I picked up the wine on the floor. Had a long slug. One of the lads in the pictures on the mantlepiece was giving me a strange look. Fifties. Flushed cheeks. A woman beside him in a flowery dress and her hair blowing in the wind. Great day out.

'Say something, Charlie. Give me something. I'm in deep here with you. I need communication. Is it to do with the shooting at the pub? I thought McWard was dead?'

'He is.'

'So, what's the problem?'

'It's somethin else now.'

'Always *something*. I need to know. What did you do? How serious is it?'

'If it goes wrong, it could mean jail. For a long time.'

'Jail? Like how long? Years? A life sentence? But that's insane, for what? Is it the money laundering?'

'That's all I can tell you. Maybe Athlone goes ok, but maybe it doesn't. I don't want to lose you but now's your chance to get out.'

'Maybe I can't. How can I? I'm in love with you.'

Her tin box was on the shelf. She opened it, said: 'I need a joint.'

She got it ready, with: 'This is not me.'

'What's not you?'

'This. This life. I don't know.'

'What *is you*, then? These pictures? Big weddings with roast beef dinners and big desserts? Cos that's not me.'

She was confused, said: 'That's not a wedding. They're

extras from a movie premiere years ago. That's not who *I am*. You're so arrogant and full of your own importance. You think you know everything. Making all these assumptions about me.'

'Who are you then?'

'Don't you know? Look at me. Don't you see me? We're living together. *Focus*. We're in a relationship. I'm a real thing. There's more to women than satisfying *your* needs. We're actual people, you know? Not tropes for your ideal view of the world.'

'What the fuck is a trope?'

'Ah shut up.'

'And half your life is on a film set somewhere that you can't talk about. How am I supposed to *know* you?'

'That's my work. My passion. I don't compromise that for you. Or for anyone.'

'So go fuckin do it. And I'll do my work. And I won't talk to *you* about it. And it'll all be fine.'

'But I don't hurt people every day. I don't damage lives. I don't need to go on the run when we're supposed to be going out for lunch.'

'And I don't have the luxury of getting paid to live in fantasy worlds. My story goes on when the camera stops rolling.'

'You think that's what I do? Like it's all just make-believe?'

'Is it not?'

'How dare you? You judge me, and my life, and the work I do, when we're debating the consequences of you murdering someone? And you think you're on the winning side?'

'Just give it a couple of weeks and see where we land.'

'Land? I need you here. With me. You can't just leave, we're not done with each other. There's more to learn. I'm not safe when you're not here. You can't just fuck me and leave me like prey to the criminal coyotes out there.'

'Learn?'

'What if someone comes here lookin for you? And you're gone, living in some granny flat off the side of a brothel in the midlands?'

'If the cops figure out I'm livin here they'll come looking

for me. I just need to get out of sight for a while. There's nothing to worry about from anybody else. You're not in any danger.'

Beat. She crossed her legs. The flare in her jeans came up above her ankle. White bra under her black shirt. Leather jacket. Gold watch.

'I don't even know who I am right now. I feel like I'm in a dangerous current and I can't escape. Everything is so volatile. Living with you, this, and did you see the papers? About that poor guy that got killed?'

'Who?'

'A guy with four kids. My cousin went to school with him. Had his throat slit in front of his daughter.'

'Didn't hear.'

'Some fucking sick people out there. Maybe it *is* time for me to leave Galway for a while. I could move to London or Australia.'

Somewhere in the house a pump sprang to life. A shadow drifted across the floor, like a solar flare through the trees. She watched it, but something else was going on behind her eyes, and then the revelation came. She looked at me sharply. 'It was *you*.'

'What was me?'

'You killed that guy, that's why you're leaving.'

'Who? What?'

'My cousin said he was an innocent eejit. Got caught up with some vicious people.'

'He was. He did.'

'And he had four children.'

'That's true, you said that.'

'It was you? You sick bastard.'

'You're not makin sense.'

'Oh my god….in front of his daughter? His 12-year-old child?'

'What was I supposed to do? Kill her too?'

'You're *admitting* it?'

'You're surprised?'

She was waiting for the punchline, the truth going through her blood like hot copper.

'I'm stunned. I know there's people like Kramer and McWard and whoever else, but this was next level, ruthless. Inhumane. Awful.'

'And necessary.'

'Was it?'

'Bit late to take it back now.'

'You're…'

She was pale, looking dizzy and nauseous.

'He was a rat. He was trying to get me sent down.'

'Explain that to his kids! His traumatized daughter. I should go to the guards and tell them.'

'I'll put that down to stress, shock, but for your own safety…'

'What? I shouldn't talk like that again?'

'Exactly.'

'Or what?'

'Just don't.'

'Are you goin to slit my throat too?'

'I'd never hurt you.'

'Shoot me?'

'No.'

'Chop me up?'

'Don't be stupid.'

The permutations were rolling out in front of her. 'But someday it'll be necessary too. I'll be an obstacle. To you, or to somebody like you. And you'll all justify my death as somehow part of your warped life, and code, and psycho needs. Another female victim in your crime dramas where you all think you're the main character. But you're all just sewer dogs possessed by the same sick evil demons. How could I be so blind? I thought you had a soul, somewhere in there, in your drunken dungeon of a mind.'

Her voice cracked. 'But you're just a coward.'

'I never said otherwise.'

'And everybody and everything around you dies or gets killed so you can survive. You're a parasite, feeding off the vulnerable, kept alive by innocent fools that are stupid enough to have faith in you.'

She was holding back tears, but her conviction was absolute.

Freddie's car beeped outside. Time to go. I stood there, nothing to say, letting our future together die, same as watching the life leave Oscar's eyes.

'That's him.'

'Goodbye, Charlie. I know all I need to know now. Go be a hero.'

And I left her crying on the couch.

Athlone

Leaving her house. Everything was sharp. The wind, the trees, like natural Cubism. I sat on the neighbour's window. Not too sure how it went so wrong, so fast. Only that she was right, there was no way back. Felt like I was on a rocky ship, a steep slant, hard to keep steady. I felt cut in half. Like the right side of my body was invisible, or I couldn't feel it, or it was torn off me. All the nerves burned like hurt. It was loss, but deeper. It was grief, but stronger. It was fear, but terror. It was the last train to a new world and she was on it, and I wasn't, and she didn't want me there. Couldn't have me there. I'd lost her, before I even knew I *had* her, and now I'd never have her again. And that meant something. And when's the last time anything meant something?

He picked me up in a nowhere Mazda. New and full of sensor lights and cameras, and it wouldn't shut the fuck up until I put on my seatbelt.

I got him to pull in at Spar and picked up a bottle of Faustino for the road. Take the edge off, level out the jangled conscience.

We went up the M6.

Oranmore, Athenry, Loughrea, breezed through the toll.

Freddie said: 'I used to live up here years ago. I'll get you a place to lay low for a while.'

He sounded far away, like he was talking through a plastic Halloween mask. Rain came down the window. Bounced like the sound of popping popcorn. It glistened and shone and sang down the glass. I wanted him to press rewind, undo, turn the car around. Anything that would get me back to Karena. But my part in her life was over, no words left in my script, time to get the fuck off the stage.

'What's it like?'

'Athlone? Great town. There'll be plenty of work up here too.'

'Fuckin Oscar. Who's comin to this meetin anyway?'

'There's a few. The Wards are up from Limerick.'

'What are they like?'

'They're ok, they like money. The leader is a fella called Joe. Last week he killed his cousin cos he owed him a Euro and he wouldn't give it. They're into weed and cocaine mostly.'

'Who else?'

'Lonergan's crew from Westmeath, the Sweeneys from Sligo, and Paddy Joyce from Dublin.'

'Anyone from the North?'

'One of the Kavanagh brothers said he'd come down.'

'What's he like?'

'Pain in the hole, but better to get him onboard.'

'How're we goin to play it?'

'They can have the drugs, we'll do any banks, debt collecting, brothels, normal shit. We'll tax anythin that comes through Galway.'

'Are you not tempted to get back into the coke yourself?'

'No. It's a rotatin presidency that ends in a grave. They can have it, as long as they pay the tax. The local guards might calm down if there's no violence, agreements in place, no more tourists shot in the head. CAB might even fuck off too.'

'What if the gangs don't agree?'

'They'd have to be stupid.'

'That's possible too.'

'Like I was sayin before. It was me that set up all the routes down the docks. I know the crews, the contacts abroad, I have a good name locally. They need me to keep things running smooth. The Columbians, The Dutch, The Moroccans, they won't work with people they don't know anymore. I can put an organised face on the whole operation. I let McWard fuck around the last while because there was nothin much happening anyway, but now everyone wants to get back in action and they need someone like me.'

'Who do you think killed him?'

'McWard? It was the Lonergan's.'

'Why?'

'He sent up some of his dealers to Tullamore. Tried selling on their patch and they wasted him.'

'Saved us a job.'

'But now we have to make a stand. They're comin down for the coke routes either way. Might aswell be on our terms or the cunts will be running around Galway like cowboys and causin more shite we don't need.' He indicated, said: 'I'm goin to have a piss here in Ballinasloe.'

We pulled in. Found a petrol station. Freddie came back, holding a white bag, asked: 'Do you want a sausage roll?'

'No.'

'They're fuckin lovely.'

He put one in his mouth, started the car, saying: 'This is one of Tommy Ryan's stations.'

'The gambler from Roscommon?'

'Yeah.'

It was small, compact. Not much going on. Useless teenager behind the counter. 'Did you look into it? The thing he was saying about washing the diesel.'

'I did.' Mumbling through the sausage roll, crumbs everywhere, he said: 'There's a fella I know in Athlone here that's interested. He has a contact in Cavan that can clean the fuel. I deal with him for the cigarettes too.'

'So how's it work?

'Green diesel, washed. Half the price. There's a pipeline from the North into a farm in Virginia where it gets converted. From there they drive it down to our man in Athlone. Then you can pick it up and distribute it to the west.'

'To Tommy's stations?'

'Yeah. How would you be fixed? Instead of bringing smokes, you can bring down the fuel and we can fill up the tanks in the likes of this place here.'

'Why doesn't someone from Cavan do it themselves? Or even from Athlone?'

'Because the west is our territory. It's a courtesy thing. And they don't want to screw up our other deals like the guns and smokes. We also know the area, the people, the geography. We start off with Tommy's six stations, then expand as we go along.'

'Will the stations even want it?'

'Well Tommy's stations will be getting it anyway. Whether they want it or not.' Beat. 'It's good money.'

'How good?'

'We buy a tank for ten grand, sell it for thirty.'

'Nice dusht.'

'But I need someone reliable that won't flip if they get caught.'

'Like me?'

'Yeah, you're different, Charlie. You're not like the rest of us.'

'How's that, Freddie?'

'You're solid as a fuckin rock. Dead woman, cop killer, dead Kramer, and you're still not in jail. You're like a fuckin cockroach in Chernobyl.'

'Mr. fuckin compliments.'

'Will you do it?'

'When's it start?'

'Today. I'll be killin all the birds I can up here. We'll have this meetin, then you can pick up the first truck. It'll be there waitin.'

'Just like that?'

'Just like fuckin that. Problem?'

'No. Fast, maybe.'

'Only way to do it. You'll be movin to Athlone tonight. I can collect your shit when I'm back down and bring it up.'

'I don't have anythin.'

'Nothin at all?'

'Not a fuckin thing.'

'Tasty monkey. It's settled then?'

I thought about Karena crying on the couch, said: 'It's settled.'

'That station back there, you'll be deliverin to it later this evenin.'

'How technical is it? I should look like I know what I'm doin.'

'Tiger Tony will fill you in.'

'Who the fuck is Tiger Tony?'

'He's the contact in Athlone.'

'Why they call him Tiger Tony?'

'Fucked with a tiger at a circus when he was a kid. Lost an arm.'

'Sounds great.'

'Don't worry. He's lived a cautious life since. You can move up here and let the Oscar thing die down. It's good grade, low profile.' He looked over at the wine, said: 'Just don't crash the fuckin truck when you're bananas.'

Tiger Tony

We took exit 13 into Monksland. Freddie establishing the geography as we went along. Saying things like: 'We'll go right here onto Connaught Street and the hotel isn't far.'

'Show me where to pick up the truck first.'

'I don't know if we'll have time.'

'Fuck them, they can wait.'

We went through St. Anne's Terrace, up through the Battery Heights and down through Pearse Street. Breezed by the cop station and over the bridge and right towards Golden Island. Drove by Aldi and hung a right behind Tesco.

There, a large forecourt. It had a Russian look, or something you might see in the dusty outback of Australia. There was no kiosk, no shop, no dickheads filling up new cars. It was more of a wholesale place for trucks. Lot of tanks around, and rusty poles, and large grates for any spills. The car hummed in, hummed lightly, observed.

'It should be a blue lookin beast, with a yellow cab.' Said Freddie.

I saw it, said: 'That's her I'd say.'

We pulled around. Windows down, the smell of fumes and wet dust. I got out, walked to the driver's side, had to climb up, pull open the door.

A smell like varnish and old cushions. Thick dirty windshield. A CB radio. *Scania* written across the steering wheel.

I put it in neutral, turned the key and she roared alive.

A worthy engine, a loyal confident surge. I revved and she reacted well, begging for more. Let it idle then, catch her breath. Then switched it off and got out.

Back on the ground, felt like I'd just left a plane. My feet thick on the cement, still light from the vibration. Sat into the nowhere Mazda, much lighter, much lower. Freddie said: 'Well she starts anyway.'

'I'll bring it down to that place tonight.'

'Yeah, Tony will meet you here later and tell ya how it works. We've a bit of work to do with persuadin the other stations because Tommy has them leased out. Shouldn't be too much hassle.'

'Tell me more about Tiger Tony.'

'He's a fixer that likes a nixer. This is an honest depot, where regular trucks come and fill up on legal diesel. But the way things are gone with VAT and tax, he wants to cut a few corners. So they bring down the green stuff from the North as far as here and store it. Then we come and fill up to supply the stations in the west. Having an open business helps laundering the money and nobody wonders why we're coming and going. We hide in plain sight.'

'And we make €20,000 profit per run after costs?'

'Yeah. Give or take.'

'How many runs?'

'Five stations. Once a week, twenty fills a month, four hundred thousand profit or nearly five million a year.'

'Fuck.'

'Fuck, yeah. Who needs cocaine, eh? Let the other fuckers kill each other and we'll be workin away here nice and quietly.'

'Tommy must have expenses too, keeping the shops open, all that.'

'He can use the income from the rest of the business.

Breakfast rolls, and coffees and fuckin teabags or whatever. I don't give a fuck what he does. We'll be knockin his debt off this gig til he's clear.'

'He's sick too.'

'Exactly. He mightn't be around for much longer so we better milk it while we can.'

I looked around, said: 'It's a big operation.'

'It is. But not as big as drugs, or guns. It's more of an honest crime, like working when you're on the dole. And the only one gettin screwed is the government, and who wants to complain about that?'

'Are you goin to tell the other gangs about it at the meetin today?'

'No, this is our own thing, side hustle. Tell them cunts nothin, especially that thick Kavanagh prick from the North, thinks he owns the place up there.'

A dose from Dublin

We went back through town in the nowhere Mazda. It had no life, no aggression, no style. Just a bubble of safety and silent cruising. I don't trust a car when I can't hear the engine. Feels like I'm not connected, disassociated, not in control. This fuckin thing was somewhere else, singing its German song, keeping us insulated, separated, built for a dead consciousness. A doctor, someone like that, someone that's never touched the void. I had another pull of the wine, got an image of my brain burning away in a smoky mess. Took another swig and felt better.

Interior. Mind. Intrusive thoughts.

I could hear the dead, their voices. El Niño's melody, Malone's tobaccoed questions, Kramer laughing.

Karena's disappointment and outrage.

I put the window down and the sounds of life came in with the Westmeath air. Athlone was vibrant, energetic. Less pretentious than Galway. Up John Broderick Street. Through Church Street and around by the Castle. A busker on the bridge playing the accordion.

We came around by Sean's Bar, up by The Snug and past The Fiddler. Turned at Walsh's Centra and found The Clover Heights.

Few big cars already there. SUVs. BMWs. All that shit.

I spotted a flashy motorbike in the corner. Suzuki, Honda, something. Asked: 'That one of us?'

'Paddy Joyce. A fuckin dose from Dublin.'

'What's he doin with the bike?'

'Says it's perfect for gettin away from guards.'

'Is it?'

'Yoke like that, yeah. Hit 200 miles an hour handy enough.'

'Do the job alright.'

'Til he hits the fuckin wall. We wouldn't be that lucky though.'

Walked in. Fancy foyer. Expensive couches. Freddie talked to the woman at the front desk.

I went to the bar. The name on the girl's tag said: **Tanya.** I ordered a triple vodka and diet coke. She frowned, looked behind me like she expected a stag party. Then she went to get it. Turned once and asked: 'Did you say *triple*?'

'I did.'

She managed it. Sparked the coke and charged me €18.50.

Paid her a twenty and threw it back. Had it downed by the time she got my change. Left the glass on the counter and said thanks, Tanya, keep it. Freddie behind me now, are ya right?

We walked down a long corridor.

Other events on too.

Mindfulness in 203.

Business Blitz in the Shannon Suite.

A Psychic Conference in the Ballroom.

A gangland coffee morning in 218.

The room had a brown table, black chairs, jugs of water. Bright windows, radiators. Plain walls. High ceiling, fluorescent lights. A bowl with UHT milk and sugar cubes. Plain grey carpet. A smell like ink or paint. We took a seat at the bottom of the table beside the door. The rest of them were already there. Freddie had given me a short breakdown on who they were on the way over.

Joe Ward was in a leather jacket, white shirt, blue jeans. Crew cut. He was known as a peacemaker, a diplomat, a negotiator that could get a deal for everyone. Things had been bad in the west. People not making money since Kramer was gone and the crackdown started. Now with McWard dead he wanted to find a new way of doing business.

John Lonergan was older than I imagined. Late forties, greying hair at the sides. Suit, coffee, legs crossed. International reputation. Ran a waste collection business. Lot of recycling abroad, plenty of contraband coming back in on his trucks. Under pressure from the guards with the Dublin and Cork routes. He needed Galway.

Derek Kavanagh stood by the window, arms folded, giving a superior vibe. He had tattoos, black boots, sleeveless white t-shirt, beard. Did time in Belfast for possession of Semtex and a botched tiger raid. Strapped a bomb to a teenage girl and told her to walk up to a British Checkpoint or he'd kill her parents. The bomb didn't go off and he got sent down. Out since under the Good Friday Agreement. Now he's here looking to go selling drugs. Fund the campaign. Help the cause.

Unite that.

Pookie Sweeney was a Traveller in a tracksuit and runners. Huge stomach and a gypsy smig. Gold rings and a holy medal around his neck. He brought a lot of weed in from England and trafficked women too. Specialised in young girls from Eastern Europe. They were promised visas, a better life, opportunity. But he kept them in poor conditions, run down houses on the outskirts of Sligo. Living in filth and squalor, like slaves. Word was he wanted to get into the coke business.

Paddy Joyce had his head down, scrolling through *Boyle Sports* on his phone. Bike helmet and gloves beside him. He was in a black leather jacket, earring, and bright blue eyes. Late thirties. Shite tattoos on his neck. Evil bastard look. Worked well with Kramer. Thick as fuck since it all went wrong. Had territory in Dublin. Felt like he was the only one that mattered.

Freddie opened with: 'Ok, men. Thanks for coming. No point fuckin around. We're all serious people, let's get down to business.'

'What do you have in mind?' Says Lonergan

'You all know me. I've worked with ye on different stunts over the years and I'm a man of my word.'

Paddy Joyce cut in, cheeky, with: 'You should have killed McWard months ago.'

'And your father should've pulled out early too but fuck all we can do about that either.'

'Were you afraid of him?'

'Let him talk, Paddy.' Said Pookie.

Joyce doesn't want to let it go, comes back with: 'All I'm sayin if someone shot up *my* pub, he wouldn't be walkin around like that.'

Lonergan comes in stern with: 'Let's get back to business.'

'Yeah, I'm not here to talk shite.' Said Kavanagh with his Northern accent.

'Only one talkin shite is Paddy the fuckhead Joyce here.' Said Freddie.

'Who're you callin a fuckhead?'

'You're not at home now, sham. I don't go up to Dublin tellin you how to run things.'

Joyce pointed to me, said: 'And what the fuck's *he* doin here?'

'What's your problem?'

'Everythin was goin alright til you went fuckin shootin everyone.'

'Nobody died that didn't deserve it.'

'And now we're all here. Sortin out your shit.'

'What do you want to do about it?'

'I'll stab you in the two eyes you culchie prick.'

'Will ya now? Not before I shove your fuckin Honda 50 up your hole.'

Lonergan said: 'Enough.'

'We're here to stop the killin.' Said Ward.

'One more do no harm.' Said Joyce.

'No harm at all.' I said.

'Outside. And I'll box your head.'

I stood up, armed with homicidal rage, said: 'Let's go.'

'Fuckin relax!' Said Freddie. 'I don't want the whole town knowin there's a crime syndicate meetin on and here's two of them havin a scrap in the fuckin car park.'

I said: 'Upgrade that scrap to a murder, Freddie.'

Joe Ward came in, laced with firm authority. 'Let's get the meetin started here. Paddy, sit down.'

'I'll call the fuckin meetin.' Said Freddie. 'Or I'll call the whole fuckin thing off and there won't be a gram of coke comin through Galway for the next ten years.'

Pookie stirred, said: 'Chill the beans, boss. Paddy, you keep your opinions to yourself unless they're important.'

'All my opinions are important. And who's talkin to you?'

'Freddie?' Cut in Kavanagh. 'Can you guarantee cargo comin through the docks? That's the only point of me being here.'

'I can organise the boats, the schedules, the same routes as before. The complicated part is how much you're going to pay me to do it.'

Lonergan shrugged, said: 'Name your price.'

'I want more than money.'

'What could you want more than money?' Asked Joe Ward.

'I want peace locally. I don't want people getting shot, stabbed, fucked over. And I don't want my own businesses interfered with.'

'What business are they?' Asked Kavanagh.

'I do all the extortion, banks, gambling, brothels, anything that's not drug related. I leave that to ye. I'll give my blessing for the routes. They trust me and they'll work with me. They can't stand the rest of ye. Especially pricks from Dublin.'

'Fuck off.' Said Paddy Joyce.

'And what'll you charge?' Asked Pookie

'A million. A month. Between ye. That's a €200,000 Each.'

'And you can guarantee safe delivery?' Asked Lonergan.

'Absolutely.'

'With no lost cargo?' Asked Kavanagh.

'There'll be some bad luck. Storms, acts of God. That'll be your loss. An odd one will be intercepted, that's the cost of doin business. But everythin else I stand over. Safe passage, safe delivery. I'll have a crew to meet whoever's comin to the docks. You come, you pick up your load and you go. You get your lunch, your drink, your women somewhere else. If there's a dispute, we meet up like this and resolve it. We don't go vigilante and start killin each other. That's what brings the cops down on us. And I don't want that shit.'

'When can we start?' Asked Joe.

'I'm ready to go in a week.'

'We could just kill you and move in.' said Paddy Joyce.

'Better men than you have tried.'

'I could have you done in time for the six o'clock news.'

'Not if I snap your neck before you make it to the door.'

'And what about our existing arrangements, Freddie?' Asked Lonergan.

'Cigarettes stay the same. Pookie, Mayo and Sligo are your territories for Coke. I'm happy to let you have Galway too but then all other income sources are mine. Your sharkin, whores, chop shops, I'll take them over so you're not hangin around like a fart in a church.'

Pookie shrugged, said: 'Suits me, easy money.'

'Why the fuck's Sweeney get Galway all to himself?' Said Joyce. 'Me and Kramer had a good deal there.'

'Well, he's not around, fuckhead. This is the new world order.'

'I don't agree to those terms.'

Pookie said: 'Then go shite in a bucket. If the man says I'm takin it. I'm takin it.'

Freddie said: 'Like I said, lads. I have enough money. It's peace I want.'

'Sounds good to me.' Said Joe Ward.

'I'll take the deal.' Said Kavanagh.

'I don't agree.' Said Paddy Joyce. 'I'm not settlin for this.'

'Let's vote on it.' Said Lonergan.

'I think it's pretty fuckin obvious.' Said Freddie. 'Everyone wants it except the dick from Dublin.'

'Fuck yourselves.' Said Paddy Joyce. 'We're not the fuckin United Nations.'

'I don't care what all you squabble about.' Said Kavanagh. 'As long as there's no interference at the border. Frankly, I think the rest of you are all fuckin scumbags.'

'Go home so and make a few bombs for yourself.' Said Pookie. 'And shove one up in your gob while you're at it.'

'I'm savin all my Semtex for the next haltin sight I see.'

'What do you mean by that?'

'He means he thinks you're a dirty fuckin knacker.' Said Paddy Joyce.

'Say it again.'

'You're a dirty fuckin scumbag tinker. Are you even *allowed* in places like this?'

'Don't worry, Paddy. I'm allowed in lots of places. And I have them words you're after sayin burnt into my head now.'

'Burn this too: you're not gettin Galway.'

'I'll meet you down there someday. And we'll see who's gettin it then.'

'We'll see alright.'

'Or I'll meet you in Dublin first.'

'Any day you like.'

'In your big house with the nice trees around it.'

Paddy's tone changed, with: 'How the fuck do you know where I live?'

'Now. See. Travellers know a lot more than you think. Goin around in your flashy bike.'

Freddie cut in, with: 'Sweeney's gettin Galway. It's decided. Paddy you're out of the west. Nobody's sayin you can't have the whole of Dublin for yourself, sounds more than fair to me.'

'It's the business we're in, Paddy.' Said Lonergan.

'This is not business.' Said Paddy. 'This is gettin fucked over. I want my old deal from Kramer's time.'

Freddie said: 'This is the deal on the table now. You don't like it. Fuck off.'

'Maybe I'll just take it.'

'Try it.' Said Pookie.

'What are you goin to do? Put a gypsy curse on me?'

'I'm happy to sacrifice some of my territory around Leinster to compensate you, Paddy. For the sake of peace and gettin back to business.' Said Lonergan.

'No. I want what's mine.'

'Them days are gone.' Said Freddie. 'You come. You go. You leave the west to the west.'

'West to the west, is it? One big happy family.' He stood up. 'I'll see ye around, men. Ye might not see me, but I'll be waiting around every dark corner. You're *all* knackers as far as I can see.'

'Go home will ya?' Said Pookie. 'You and your tricycle outside.'

'We're not finished.'

Pookie blew him a kiss as he walked out.

'Don't worry.' Said Lonergan. 'I'll talk to him.'

'He's a prick, Johnny.' Said Freddie. 'He always was. And he's causin shite here for nothin.'

'I'm his gateway to the Midlands. He'll listen to me. He's just trying to act big today.'

Joe Ward, said: 'So everyone else agreed? Derek?'

'Like I said: as long as nothin interrupts my operations on the border, I'm happy.'

'Pookie?'

'I'm a 100%. Except can you do any better than €200,000? Would you settle for €190,000 instead? Throw a bitta luck into it?'

'No. And fuck yourself for askin. John? You happy?'

'Absolutely. It should have been sorted out months ago.'

There was a roar outside as Paddy's motorbike took off. Everyone ignored it.

Freddie continued: 'I'll make arrangements for the money to be picked up. Any late payments and I'll have your coke confiscated and shared with everyone else here. Have your payments ready each month, stick to the rules and there won't be any need to meet again.'

'Thank fuck for that.' Said Kavanagh. 'Are we finished?'

'I'll be in touch.' Said Freddie.

Pookie stood up, turned to Kavanagh, said: 'I'll remember you too, bomber-boy.'

'Go traffic a Polish child you pikey cunt.'

Pookie walked to the door, turned and said: 'I might. Or maybe I'll just come for yours. Two girls, is it? And a boy? Bye now Gerry Adams.'

And he walked out.

'Fuckin hate knackers.' Said Kavanagh.

War within a month

After they left, Freddie said: 'What do you think?'

'I think there'll be war within a month.'

'If there is, it was comin anyway. Lonergan might hold it together.'

'I wouldn't trust him at all.'

'I don't trust him either. But he needs the routes so that'll keep manners on him.'

'Give him nothin. No details or contacts. That's what he wants, then he'll try and cut you out.'

'Yourself and Paddy got off to a good start.'

'Prick.'

'He's a dog. Never mind him.'

'I should have fuckin opened his throat.'

'Except you're tryin to lay low. Killin Dublin drug dealers probably doesn't fit into that category.'

'What are we goin to do if he kicks off in Galway?'

'Let's see if Lonergan can rein him in first.'

'Don't be lettin that shit go.'

'What do you want me to do?'

'If it was up to me he'd be in the Shannon already.'

'Fuckin Ted Bundy. Give peace a chance, sir.'

'Peace is for pussies. Did you get me a house?'

'I did. We'll go there now.'

It was a bedsit on the westside, just off Battery Heights. Spare and clean. We walked in, smell of polish and paint. Telly in the corner, kettle on the locker. Like a hotel room you could live in, but a far cry from Karena's.

'What do you think?'

'It'll do.'

'It's perfect. Quiet neighbours, good area. No need to draw attention to yourself.'

'Where's the nearest off-licence?'

'You've a run to do with the truck first?'

'Oh, yeah.'

'I'll ring Tony and tell him you're comin. Leave it until after eight in case the customs are out. After that, she's all yours.'

'You headin back to Galway?'

'I am. We're opening the pub next week. Need to get it stocked and ready. Did a full refurb, she's lookin nice.'

'What about CAB?'

'The accountant swung it, money can't be traced back to me.'

'Tasty.'

'Even got my dole again and the ex is happy cos her payments are back too. Gettin the young lad for the day tomorrow. He wants to go on the train. Need to get his conductor outfit washed.'

'How much the pub cost to get fixed up?'

'Nearly thirty grand and the insurance is gone high as fuck, but great publicity.'

'How do you mean?'

'Place is notorious now. Half the city will be down takin selfies.'

'At least McWard was good for somethin.'

'Shitebag. Let me know how you get on with the truck.'

Great life altogether

Exterior. Athlone. Evening. The air was sweet with the fumes of open fires. I could almost taste the turf. The dominant colour was acrylic, a twilight from the calm midlands sky. I found Connaught Street. Walked up by Walsh's pub, two charity shops and a bookies. Found the off-licence on the right-hand side.

Beauty personified. Dutch Gold, Orchard Thieves. Wine everywhere. I knew I'd be driving so kept it calm for now. Went for a naggin of vodka and a six pack of Linden Village. Then said I better have a bottle of Brandy for the house later.

Tall fella behind the counter. Tinted glasses. Totted it up and I paid him. He said: 'Nice evenin.'

'Not bad. What time do ye close?'

'Around ten. But there's a pub next door if you want a pint after that.'

Drank the naggin on the way home. Got to the bedsit, sparked a can, took a hit. On the run, bedsit in Athlone, night coming, Karena gone, bag of drink. Great life altogether.

The truck

Later, I went to get the truck. It was dark now, except for a fluorescent glow from the shopping centre across the road. The yard was empty, quiet. Got to the driver side of the Scania and hopped in.

Same scene. Thick windshield. CB radio.

Heard a knock on the window. Turned around. There was a fella standing there. Old, wizened, missing two bottom teeth. Scarecrow look. Old flannel shirt, blue jeans, loose boots. Eyes like murky lake water.

'Howya, Charlie.'

'Who are you?'

He pointed at the stub, said: 'I'm the one-armed bandit. Freddie rang to say you're takin a load this evenin.'

'Down to Ballinasloe. That alright?'

'Sound by me. I just topped up this one today. Ye're fast operators.'

'No point leavin it sittin around.'

'True. Do you know what you're doin?'

'Not a clue.'

'Better show you how to fill it, so. Hop out.'

The ground frizzled, my feet drinking evil karmic nutrients and dangerous cosmic vibrations. Followed Tony around to the side. He pointed under the truck. There was a hose there, locked in by a thick chain. He said: 'You have to take that out and you're looking for a cover on the ground like this....'

He pointed to a hatch beside the back wheel. Two grips either side to twist it off. He handed me a pair of gloves, said: 'Anti-clockwise.'

I bent down, gave it some love. It was hard and awkward but eventually relented. It was like a deep black cave full of diesel.

'You'll be looking for one of those at each station. It's what supplies the pumps. You take your hose here, lock it around the grooves and start fillin.'

'How do I get it flowin?'

'These taps here.'

He tapped a rusty lever. 'Pull it down to fill, push it up to stop. There's a sensor on it anyway that knows when it's gettin near the top and it'll cut itself off. Try not to mix the green with the red. It's best to have a separate hatch for these deliveries.'

'I'll ring Tommy and tell him to have it sorted.'

'I don't need names or anythin else. You can store it here and that's where I stop askin questions.'

'How do I fill the truck?'

'See them tall cylinders over there? Same principle. But instead of putting it into the ground, you attach it here to the side. I'll show you, c'mon.'

Light shaky streetlight from across the road, aeonic and warm. Tony's grey hair slightly disturbed by the mild wind. My ears were ringing, the vodka singing. I wanted a smoke but one spark around here and it's Apocalypse Athlone.

Tony pointed to a hatch on the side of the tank.

'Same thing. Anti-clockwise. We attach the pipe from the storage tanks but don't worry, I can get that sorted my side. I just want the stuff in, out and gone.'

'Did ya talk money with Freddie?'

'Yeah, that's all done. We probably don't need to meet again.'

Niamh

Went out the Ballymahon road and cruised down the bypass.

Called Tommy Ryan. He answered hoarse with: 'Hello?'

'Tommy, it's Charlie.'

'Charlie.'

'I'm comin to Ballinasloe with the first load.'

'Ok. I can't make it tonight. I'm very weak.'

'I'll be there in half an hour.'

'Bu…'

'Just fuckin be there.'

I hung up. Sparked a can. Drank deep. My vision swayed. Rasped and accelerated. Clear road ahead. Squeaking springs on the seat. Gave it throttle, trying to outrun myself. Hit the radio. They were talking shite about the arts. Ireland's booming film industry. Oscar season coming up. Reminded me too much of Karena. Tried the other stations. Found The Black Keys *Things Ain't Like They Used To Be.* Let that roll, assimilate the scene, slow the warp down.

More Linden Village. Felt the mind bend. Pressure, a darkness, an invisible weight, like a boot leaning into my brain. Changed gear, surged on. Another mile, another string of connected moments, another spent token of drunken time.

Got to Ballinasloe. Off the Shannonbridge exit and faced for the town centre. Trucked by Dolan's and turned left and found the place.

No sign of Tommy. Said I'd give it a few more minutes.

Same scene as Roscommon. Different young one behind the counter, working hard on her phone, getting upset by customers.

Her tag said: **Niamh.**

I told her: 'I'm here to fill the tanks.'

'Of the petrol?'

'The diesel.'

'Ok. Whatever….'

And she threw a set of keys on the counter.

Handy enough.

Exterior. Forecourt in Ballinasloe. Briquettes. Barrels of gas, bags of coal, oil, car batteries, all that shite.

On the street, mothers wearing pyjamas walked by, pushing prams and smoking. All up, things were calm, not much happening, like a social glacier drifting in the arctic silence.

Found a hatch like Tony was telling me. Padlocked.

Four keys on the bunch from Niamh. Tried them. None of them worked. Big fuckin surprise.

Then Tommy arrived, in a battered Ford Focus. He got out, looking shook, pale, thinner, arm in a sling, said: 'That's the wrong one.'

'Nice car.'

'I prefer the Lexus. Come over here.'

We walked around the corner. More valves and plenty of space for parking. 'The cap you're looking for is here. Only ever use this one. I'll be inside. Use the yellow key.'

I drove round and attached the pipe. Pulled the lever and let her fill.

It took a while. I sparked a smoke, kept it away from the pumps. Pulled another can, ravaged it. Darker out, the dying of the light. Thought about Karena. The smell of her neck, like cosy innocence. Her grip around me in the night. Maybe there's a silver bullet, a way to turn it all around. Oscar's daughter in the kitchen…

A warning bell sounded. Tank full. I packed it all away. Went inside. Tommy was in an office out the back. Filing cabinets, paper punches, a computer with an orange ball floating around the screen.

He was sitting in the swivel chair, arranging folders.

'How'd it go?' He asked, wheezing.

'Done.'

'Great, so we're in business?'

'Yeah. We'll be expectin payment by the end of the month.'

'Of course.'

'And we'll be visiting your other stations this week.'

'I've explained to Freddie they're on a lease, but he said he'll find a way around it.'

'We will. Don't worry.'

He smiled, deathly pallor, demonic almost, asked: 'Still dead inside?'

'Same as it ever was. Have you long left?'

'Six months, at best.'

'We better get busy so.'

'Some days I still think it's all goin to be ok.'

He sounded like he wanted a sympathetic ear. So I dodged that and asked: 'What's the difference with the normal and the green diesel.'

'Nothin.'

'Well, it's a different fuckin price for a start.'

'Well, there's that, yeah.'

'And it's a different colour.'

Some life came back into his face, like the expertise gave him the chance to forget. He took on the teacher role. 'You're being too technical, Charlie. It's the same product. There's a discount on diesel that's used for agricultural purposes. So, they make it green to tell the difference.'

'And what happens when the customs pull me up and say hey, why's this shit green?'

'It'll be washed in Cavan so it'll be the same colour, just half the price. Costs the taxpayer about €800 million a year.'

'How's it get washed?'

'It gets pumped full of silicon dioxide. The process takes about two hours and suddenly you have a tank that was worth €10,000 worth three times the price. Same liquid. Same use. But immensely more valuable. There's even small-scale gangs in the North doing it in the back of Hi-Ace vans. It's now thought one in every eight litres of Irish diesel is laundered like this.'

'Why does the news say it damages cars?'

'That's the silicon dioxide again. When the engine heats up, the residue of the dioxide can solidify and cause problems. Insurance doesn't even cover it. Relatively rare though.'

'Relatively?'

He shrugged, said: 'I drive petrol mostly, so I have no personal experience.'

'Why didn't you get into it before?'

'I had plenty of opportunities. You need to know all about it when you're in this business, but I was always wealthy and did things right. Until now.'

He winced in pain, held his stomach, his eyes going wide like this might be the big one. Then he looked up, asked: 'Do you need anythin else?'

'Not for now. Good luck.'

Exterior. Forecourt. Spotted the storeroom open. Helped myself to a carton of smokes and a bottle of JD. Threw them in the passenger side and got ready for the road. Next thing I spotted the cops at the pumps.

Charlie wanted for murder down in Galway, how are ya fixed? And here he is robbing storerooms. My heart skipped. I was sure Tommy had pulled a stunt, rang them. They got out, looked at me briefly, then one of them started filling and the other went inside.

They were only there as customers.

Thank fuck.

I started the engine. Kept the movements calm. Seatbelt, checking mirrors. Road conscious. The cop was still filling, getting the last drop in. Gave me a once over as I pulled out. I waved and indicated for the motorway. He nodded back, like we're all in the same over-worked game, and walked inside.

On the relieved motorway, I checked the rearview in case they had twigged something, a part of the cop's instinct might have recognized my face, or the likes of me, enough to pull me over for a routine check. But there was no sirens coming, no blue lights of the killer's disguise, just the road ahead and my new bedsit waiting.

I thought about Karena again. The dusk in Galway. The ocean's song, like a lullaby into a night of tender passion. Then the engine faltered a bit, got uncertain, like it was unsure about the direction. So I shoved it up a gear, lit a stolen smoke and sparked the bottle of JD.

Peace in our time

Freddie got busy in Galway. He paid the cops to calm down on the Oscar thing until we could find an angle, a way to get to the mother, or the daughter, and make them drop the case.

After that he set up the deals at the docks. Same routine as Kramer's time. Same payoffs, same schedules, same routes. The difference was quantity. Lonergan had expanded exponentially and needed more coke than anyone. And Pookie Sweeney was booming in Sligo and that meant more traffic. More traffic meant more risk and more bribes. It took negotiation, but he got the price right and everyone got what they wanted. The guards would ignore the late-night boats and ease off on our ordinary crimes. In return, Freddie guaranteed no gangland violence in the city. No tourists killed in pubs or grannies shot through letterboxes. It was peace for everyone. The guards on the take knew that coke was inevitable. There was too much money to be made. You could fight it and watch the town burn, or you could embrace it, have a simpler life, and get rich doing it. And once the papers weren't running blood spattered headlines about drug feuds it made no difference to anyone else. It was a perfect situation and it worked as long as everyone stayed rational.

I was surprised Paddy Joyce hadn't kicked off but Freddie said Lonergan had him under control. Sweeney was working Galway and there was no problems. Joe Ward was doing his thing in Limerick and we heard nothing from the IRA fuckhead up in the North.

I was getting notions of moving back to Galway. Everything at the bedsit smelled like stale cider and diesel.

Maybe I'd convince Karena to give it another go. Fuck it. I missed the craic at the pub too.

Then.

Loud knocking. Pink Floyd vibes. *"Time to go…."*

'Charlie? It's Freddie, open the fuckin door!'

Blinded by the light, I said: 'What?'

He walked in, blue denim jacket, furry collar. 'We have to sort out the rest of Tommy's stations.'

'Alright to get dressed first?'

'Chop fuckin chop.'

He stared at the empty cans, the ashtray, everything a mess, said: 'Jesus, you're worse than my alcoholic uncle down in Tipperary.'

'Piss off.'

My head was full of noise, half clipped conversations, bits of music, self-hatred and fear.

He took a seat, said: 'There's a situation in Galway.'

The rabid dog in me growled.

'What kind of situation?'

'Karena's gone.'

Melting dread, I said: 'Gone?'

'Gone.'

'Dead?'

He blinked, said: 'No. She fucked off somewhere. But her whole place is wrecked. Looks a bit like here.'

'Who the fuck did that?'

'Paddy Joyce. He knows a few mongs around town and called in a favour.'

'I fuckin knew he'd try somethin. Did they hurt her? Was she there? Jesus Christ, Freddie, wake up, you're like the fuckin

Dalai Lama over there. Why aren't we halfway to Dublin to wipe the floor with the cunt?'

'Calm down, Chuck Norris. I talked to Lonergan. She wasn't home. They just bust up the house and left. We're doubling Paddy's tax this month. He tries anythin else, he's all yours.'

'Did you go mute at the end of that sentence? I didn't hear the bit where we break his legs.'

'It's business, bro. Things are runnin smooth, let's not let our dicks dictate us into a nuclear holocaust. She's ok, remember? She's alive. Probably on a plane somewhere. Take the win.'

'Fuck the win. I want to see him hanging from the trees in Eyre Square.'

'It's handled. He took his shot, and he's on a yellow card, and he won't fuck up again. He's embarrassed at losing Galway and wanted to make a statement. Now it's time to de-escalate.'

'More like decapitate. What's the place look like? How bad is it?'

'Like I told ya, Crash Bandicoot on acid. Records smashed, furniture torn open. They even went through all her clothes and underwear, just to be ignorant about it. She has nice knickers in fairness, I seen them on the floor.'

My rage melted into the concrete certainty of revenge.

'I'm not happy Freddie.'

'So take a fuckin Prozac, life's not a fairy tale. If I thought they hurt her then I'd have Paddy buried to the head and stoned. For now, I have to stand over my word and guarantee the peace.'

'Where'd she go?'

'I don't know, Charlie. Her being incognito made it hard to ask her.'

'There must be some clue. What were you doin there?'

'She was supposed to work last night. Never showed up. I called over and the door was hanging off the hinges and she was Maddie McCann. Didn't hand in her notice either. She can forget her last week's pay for that.'

He lit a joint. Smelled like olive oil and roses. Reminded me of Karena smoking at Devon Park, our own private Eden. The fear was working her magic, dreaming up the scenarios, the scenes, Karena screaming with a gang around her. I found a bottle of brandy on the floor. Tore into it. Burnt the brutality of the morning, offered some fragile hope.

'You're sure she wasn't there?'

'Positive. I asked around. Banged a few heads in case Lonergan was lying. Looks like she came home yesterday, saw the scene, and hit the road.'

'I shoulda brought her up here with me.'

'I'm not sure this would be her scene, sir.'

'Not my scene either, this is Oscar's fault.'

Found my belt, put on my jeans. Hands shaking. Violent compulsions roaring.

'My ex was the same when she left with the young lad. She knew in her heart an animal like you would come in the back door one day and she got out before it happened. Karena was lucky they didn't find her home. You can't trust scumbags around a vulnerable woman any more than dogs around a baby. She's gone. Face it, she got out in time.'

I tried her phone. Straight to voicemail.

'What if they're lying? What if she's in the river?'

'She's gone, Charlie. Don't be fuckin foolin yourself. She deserves better and she knows it. She can look back in ten years when she's married to a doctor, or she'll make it at the actin shite, and she can talk about her time being a gangster's moll. But she's only goin one way now, as far as she fuckin can away from you. Don't fuck up her life because you think you're entitled to her, whether she wants you or not. She got off light, a cheap warning, and she's too smart to stay around. The more you follow her, the more trouble you bring to her door. Remember how Sonny Corleone got shot at the tolls? Let's remember to play the long game. If you're stuck for a ride you're better off with Lucy at the brothel. She's more of our kind.'

'There's more to it. I can feel it in my bones.'

'What you're feelin is finality. The spinal cord between you and her has snapped. And there's no fixin it. It's over with her. This is it, my friend. This is as good as it gets. Weed, and bedsits, and Benson for breakfast, washed down by a dash of Brandy. We don't get to keep girls like Karena. It's social gravity. People like her float up and we're kept down here, grovellin for the scraps from the upper-class tables. The whole game is rigged. End of story. Now. You ready to go? We have to fuck some people up.'

Chicken Roll

Freddie drove. I drank brandy and tried Karena again. No answer. The image of the bastards in Devon Park was going through me like sharp poison, cutting all my nerves. We had to take Lonergan's word that she was safe. If she wasn't, we'd be faced for Dublin now, and I'd be driving.

The first station was in Loughrea.

A smell like plastic and cardboard. Coffee machine choking in the corner. Spotty fella called Darren behind the counter.

Asked for the manager.

He arrived.

His name was Ger.

Shirt. Name tag. Black shoes. Holding a chicken roll.

He pulled a face like a nervous barman, said: 'Lads?'

Freddie said: 'We're here to take over.'

'Take over?'

'Yeah.'

'Are ye from….Texaco? Topaz?'

'Tommy said it's ok.'

'Tommy?'

'Ryan.'

'Oh.'

He looked over at Darren, like it was all his fault. 'I might need to ring Tommy.'

'You don't need to ring anyone.'

'I'm not sure what this is lads…but.'

I said: 'It's simple. We're takin over. You're gone.'

'I have a lease.'

'It's finished.'

'There's another year left?'

'We'll be closing that out today.'

'You can't. It's a contract. I'm due a payment if it finishes early.'

Freddie asked: 'How's Michelle?'

'Michelle?'

'Michelle. Your wife. We were out by your place this morning.'

'What the fuck're you talking about?'

'She was gettin the kids ready for school.'

Ger went pale then. Dread taking hold.

'Ring the guards, Darren.'

I said: 'Darren, how's your mother? Kathleen, is it? I seen her out walking the dog last night.'

Ger quit his lease an hour later.

The next one was in Athenry, then Mountbellew and on to Oranmore. We knew the name of every manager, his routine, family names and address. Same for every employee, cleaner and even weekend staff. We left nothing to chance. If anyone fucked around we'd be at their house that evening. Break a window, fire a shot outside, approach the wife in the supermarket. Word went around that Tommy had got into bother with serious people, and he was taking back the shops to pay his debts. Any complaints to the cops were easy to bribe away and nobody suspected the diesel scam. It was the best money I'd ever made, and nobody knew a thing about it.

Joey Juju

An odd night, I'd sneak back to Galway. Spend an evening with Lucy, let the rain dream, the music play, our bodies tire together in cum, sweat and abandon. In her bed after, she'd light a joint, watch the ceiling through the smoke, and the shadows from the headlights drifting by. Her room was on the top floor and the windows weren't sealed and the cold always got in, announcing the oceanic bite, like an old friend, a salute from the timeless sea.

Tonight, as she smoked, I put my hand between her legs, found her clit, massaged it, asked her: 'Where do you get your gear?'

She looked over, glistening lips, blonde hair obscuring her eyes.

'Why? Are you getting into the game?'

She was wet now, hummed with pleasure. 'No. I'm just wondering who's supplyin? It's supposed to be a fella from Sligo.'

She took another drag, exhaled philosophically, rolled her eyes in surrender, said: 'It's not, it's a Joyce guy from Dublin.'

'Paddy Joyce? What's he doin down here?'

She shrugged, tipped some ash into a glass beside the bed, said: 'I don't know. His cousin works for him.'

'Who's the cousin?'

She reached down, took my hand in hers, set the pace with her thin fingers over mine. Slow rhythms, musical movement, her body warm now, juddering. 'Joey Juju.'

'That's his name?'

'Yeah. I have his number if you want it.'

She rolled over on top of me, took me in her hands, massaged me, used all her tricks, skills, and intimate erotic knowledge to get me throbbing.

'Maybe tomorrow.' I said.

Morning comes like a new war, a new dawn into another battle. I looked over at Lucy. She had her back to me. Red bra, a mole on her shoulder, a smell like cocoa butter. She was sleeping sound, like she felt safe. I got up, found my clothes, felt steady, like we were a married couple and I was going out to work. A driving job, or working on a site laying blocks, and the kids next door, and the mortgage coming round. But then the moment left, like a shadow across a parallel world we'd never know, and the shakes kicked in, and I needed a drink. Always the same drunk roundabout.

Exterior. Outside her room. Walked down the stairs, a smell like mould and latex and talcum powder. The other doors were closed, quiet now.

Outside, it was back to business. Bought a bottle of Jim Beam and rang Freddie. Told him the craic about Joey Juju.

He asked me to meet the prick and get the story.

I said no fuckin problem.

Later in McMahons, just off Mainguard Street. Small crowd, open fire, soccer on the telly. A smell like hot garlic bread. I threw back three fast pints and they steadied me up, warped sense into the dark evening.

Joey came in, said: 'Howya, Charlie.'

He was in blue jeans and an orange hoodie. Warped teeth and going bald. Dark navy eyes, dirty runners.

'Don't act like we're friends.'

'Sure, we're all the one.'

'Does Pookie Sweeney know you're dealin in Galway?'

'Sweeney's a knacker. Who cares what he thinks?'

'I do, Joey. I do.'

He took a seat, confident, like this wasn't a big problem.

'Well, you're not in the game. Paddy says that's the arrangement. We take the drugs, you and Freddie take everythin else.'

'Well tell Paddy he's a fuckin dreamer.'

'We had a good set up here with Kramer. We're already established. Pookie isn't.'

'Kramer's dead. So Galway belongs to Pookie Sweeney now. Peace in our time. That's what was agreed.'

He smirked, said: 'I'll say it to Paddy.'

'You won't say it to him. You'll tell him. You're finished dealin around the city.'

He frowned now, with: 'What am I supposed to tell my customers?'

'Tell them you don't have it.'

'I'm Joey Juju. I always have it. That's what they call me. When you need your Juju, you call Joey. Coke, weed, whatever, I'm your one-stop-shop. Even in a drought.'

'Well anymore they're goin to call Pookie.'

'Who wants to be buyin off the tinkers? They sell nothin but dogshit. I even have my own Juju growhouse, top quality gear.' He reached into his pocket, said: 'Here, I'll give you a free sample.'

I slapped his hand away and the weed went across the floor. 'Tell Joyce what happened here and get the fuck out.'

He got all offended, picked up his Juju, said: 'Fuck you too, Charlie. It's a public place. Why don't you get out?'

I smashed the pint glass off the counter and went for him. Caught his ear as he was running out the door. He was like a scared animal, knocking chairs, pushing customers, demented as he looked for an escape. There was shouts, protests at spilled drink and the outrageous disruption. The shard had a nice blotch of blood and flesh on it when I sat back down, the rest of the pub were looking at me but knew better than to say anything. Fella working there gave me a pint on the house.

Fuckin hate dealers, he said.

You're a dinosaur, Charlie.

Paddy Joyce had been acting the bollox, seeing how we'd react, and he'd gotten his answer. After what I did to Joey Juju, the word went around not to sell unauthorised in the city and there was a sense of calm and structure. I went back to Athlone and let the routine kick in.

Freddie got Tommy's last station opened up - the one me and Oscar had robbed. So now it was six deliveries. Monday for Oranmore. Tuesday for Athenry, Wednesday for Loughrea. Thursday for Mountbellew, Friday for Athlone and Saturday for Galway City. We didn't have the same surveillance as the coke trade. The honest cops were focused on catching the dealers. They saw the diesel as a lesser crime, lesser scourge. We weren't directly involved but collected the tax for the routes and cleaned up on our other operations.

Then it got fucked. I was driving down the road, drinking a nice naggin of Jameson, good burn, decent escape. Listening to Guns 'n Roses, *Civil War,* feeling it on every nerve, like the musical wine of truth. "Did you wear a black armband, when they shot the man that said peace could last forever...?"

The truck was sounding good, Axl Rose even better. The windscreen was bright with the afternoon sun, and I was surfing the hit of good money, like a win at the bookies. It was outside Mountbellew, on the bog road, when the red BMW overtook me. I thought it was a boy racer, destined for the wall and an early grave. Then it cut me off and skidded to a smoky stop.

I geared down, slowed, navigated the momentum of the engine before hitting the brakes. Last thing I wanted was a jack-knife, or worse, spill the whisky.

The door opened. The glint of a gloved hand on a cocked trigger. They'd be coming for me on the driver's side. This is it, me and Slash checking out, fighting for the promised land. First, I was relieved, then thought: fuck that.

I had the Glock in the glovebox. Went for it.

A knock on the window. Too late, Charlie, the blast will be coming next. I was expecting a balaclava and cold eyes. I thought of Karena. Her warmth in the bed, the smell of her hair, the tender map of her nipple.

It took me a second to recognize him, then I saw the bandage on his ear and the picture came together.

It was Joey Juju.

What the fuck?

I rolled down the glass, said: 'What?'

He was trying to look tough in a black leather jacket, said: 'We're takin this load as compensation.'

'Compensation for what? Chopping off your thick lug?'

Another big fucker was standing on the road, sunglasses, tracksuit, holding a shotgun. He didn't look like much, a cheap extra on a day they were badly stuck.

Juju was trying to sound confident, but he was unsure of his lines, like a shite actor. He continued with: 'You stop us earning, we're entitled to make it back.'

The truck was still going, impatient and loud. 'You deal your gear in the right place and we do the rest. That's the plan.'

He looked over to make sure the other lad was still there, looked back and said: 'Says *you.* Out. C'mon. If Paddy says we're takin this truck, then we're takin this truck. Do you want me to shoot ya? Right here?'

'I want you to fuck off, I'm busy.'

He held up his shotgun, sawn-off shite, said: 'You're a dinosaur, Charlie. Time to catch up with the modern age.'

'Is that what Paddy Joyce told ya?'

'The future's here. We're goin nationwide. You, Freddie, the west, you're all gone.'

'You're goin nowhere if you pull the trigger on that fuckin thing beside a tank full of diesel.'

He looked uncertain, said: 'C'mon, get out.'

'I will, yeah.'

Civil War was over and *Get in the* Ring was going loud. A perfect soundtrack as I hit the accelerator. Felt the angry surge. The engine roared like a T-Rex and went straight into the big haystack with the sunglasses. Welded him against the BMW. He looked surprised, then shocked, then roared in pain. There was a wonderful sound of screeching metal and a satisfying crunch of bones.

Get in the ring.

Get in the ring.

Get in the ring.

Juju was shouting: 'Charlie! What the fuck're you doin?'

I backed back. Let the body fall on to the road, took aim, then ran him over him right. Made sure to catch his head.

After, the engine purred, like it was saying *what next?*

I hopped out.

Juju was looking lost, vulnerable, scared.

He was stepping backwards, said: 'Don't do it, Charlie.'

The walls either side were hand built with big stones. I walked over, took my time, picked one that felt good. Joey had never killed anyone. Never even pulled a trigger. He was middle class. Dogsbody for Paddy Joyce. Too much Scarface as a child. A coked-up fraud that didn't belong. He was frozen now, uncertain, mostly afraid. I pulled the gun off him and fucked it into the field. Held up the rock as he cried and said: 'Please….'

Ballistic

Freddie went ballistic. Called Joyce and he didn't answer.

He was due a shipment, so we called the docks and told them to hold back.

He wasn't long ringing then.

'Where the fuck's my gear?'

'Who do you think you are attackin my truck?'

'Charlie attacks my dealer in Galway, what am I supposed to do?'

'The prick shouldn't have been there - *what am I* supposed to do?'

'I don't need your permission every time I want to sell a fuckin ten spot.'

'That's the thing, dickhead. In Galway, you do. It's Pookie Sweeney's turf now.'

'If Sweeney wants to come at me, he can. It has nothin to do with you.'

'I guarantee the peace. This is your last chance. You play by the rules or you're out of the west.'

'My boys are down there now. That load better be ready in an hour.'

'I'll burn it first.'

Pause, then: 'Suit yourself. And tell Charlie he's a fuckin dead man for what he did to Joey.'

'You can tell him yourself. He's listenin.'

'Howya, Paddy.' I said.

'I'll fuckin give you "howyas."'

'How's Joey the fuckhead Juju?'

'You can ask him yourself soon enough.'

'Belt away. You dopey Dublin cunt.'

And he hung up.

Government debate on crime

That evening, there was an explosion at the docks. Ships damaged, two people killed. One of them a student. Worse still, one of the boats sank and there was bags of coke left floating all over the water.

Good man, Joyce, you fuckin eejit.

The cops went mad.

The papers went mad.

It was highlighted in a fuckin government debate on crime.

All Freddie's businesses came under a media microscope. The cops kept raiding the pub, hassling him on the street. Arresting him for anything they could, just to make it look good, like they were doing something.

I was drinking vodka at the flat in Athlone when he rang me, with: 'I talked to Lonergan.'

I took a slug, let it cut, asked: 'What did he say?'

'Says Joyce had a point, we ran his dealer out of Galway. Then you killed him.'

'What about the deal with Pookie Sweeney?'

'Says nobody cares because he's a Traveller. It was between them – until we got involved.'

'He's playin a different tune than he was at the meetin.'

'He's takin their side now. Thinks we're weak, doesn't want to pay the tax this month, waiting to see if we survive at all. Any more trouble on the diesel routes?'

'Not since Joey cried for his mother. Any luck with the Oscar thing?'

'Not a hope for now. Stay out of Galway but keep the trucks singing up there. They're the only thing bringing in any money until we get this other shite sorted. When's the next one?'

'Tomorrow.'

'Gimme a shout after. Right, I'll go.'

'G'luck.'

I hung up. Frazzled silence. The bottle almost empty. I left the phone on the bed and went to the window. Lit a smoke and watched the traffic. Dim evening, cold. The flat feeling small, the walls looking dangerous, like they might put me in a vice of bad decisions and cancerous regret.

Interior. Vinny's pub. Athlone. Connaught Street. Pictures of Elvis and Marilyn Monroe on the wall. Lynyrd Skynyrd on the jukebox singing *Freebird.* Lifers at the bar, making noise, talking shite about politics, sport, going to the bog. Girl behind the counter has long black hair and moves like she knows what she's doing. I got flashbacks of Karena, painful panic, like I missed my exit a hundred miles ago. Neutered that, ordered a cider. She smiled as she left down the change, bright blue eyes in the dark pub light. A pale imitation of the real thing, a hologram of the fading past, her ghost on another timeline.

Punctured the pint, enjoyed the dead apples, and the ethanol chorus. Another hit and it was gone. Gave her the shout for a refill. She pulled the tap and it flowed like cold magma, or the addict's bright gold.

My phone rang. A northern accent with: 'Alright, Charlie boy?'

'Who the fuck is this?'

'We met in Athlone a while back there, aye?'

'Kavanagh?'

'I'll not be sayin names over the phone, sir. Just let it be clear who you're dealin with.'

'What do you want?'

'Did you think you can be takin diesel over the border like that with no consequences?'

'It's got nothin to do with you.'

'We tax border trade, son. So, aye, it's got a lot to do with us.'

'And what do you want?'

'Our cut.'

'We're already lettin you though Galway.'

'You never mentioned the smugglin.'

'Then how'd ya find out?'

'What's that matter? I made it clear I didn't want my operations up here interfered with.'

'How much you lookin for?'

'We'll take over the Athlone and Mountbellew stations. They're the closest to us here. You can keep the rest. For now.'

'Just like that?'

'Just like that. And we'll need a cut from the Ballinrobe job.'

'What Ballinrobe job?'

'Don't insult me, Charlie. Ye pricks went down and busted out an ATM and claimed it was our operation. Let's call it 20k. Mate's rates. But any more surprises and we'll be speaking again and it won't be as pleasant the next time, I can assure you of that, aye.'

The line went dead, bomb threat style.

I was getting annoyed now.

Freddie got arrested

Freddie got arrested. I was in Vinny's when I saw it on the telly. RTE job. Breaking News. Freddie in handcuffs. Significant blow to the criminal fraternity. A guard talking to the camera, saying it was part of an investigation into loan sharking, sex trafficking and energy fraud. Didn't know what the fuck he meant by *energy fraud*. Then he held up one of the gammy magnets, said: 'If you're using one of these, you're breaking the law, and you can be sure we'll find you.'

One of the gang was also "...sought in relation to a murder investigation..." That meant me. Fuck. They'd be at my door next. Said I better get a hotel just in case. If Joey Juju had found me, anyone could.

Booked into The Creggan that evening. Took a room on the ground floor, close to an exit door. Double bed, locker, lamp, telly, kettle, sachets of coffee and shite milk.

Broke out a bottle of Jamaican Rum. It was like potent seawater with a stallion's kick. Turned on the TV, no updates on the news, let the mind ruminate, figure out what to do. I thought back on the day at The Clover Heights. Pookie Sweeney and Kavanagh at each other like dogs. Decided it might be worth a look.

Same Smig

Exterior. Halting Site. Sligo. Found it up a dirt road. Pushed open the hollow gate. Five caravans in the middle of the field. Rusty barrels and tyres left around. A white cat tearing open bags of rubbish. Lit a smoke, walked over, through the smell of stale shit and grass, listening to the shouts of the kids, and the noise of the adults. They talked in mild arguments, empty threats, questions that sounded like accusations. The women sat in fold up chairs, watching me, smoking. They were in nightclothes, and slippers, with frizzy hair, and suspicious eyes. I gave a nod but they showed no recognition, just waited for me to play my hand.

Pookie was sitting beside a campfire. Children running around him, screaming, fighting, threatening each other. He told them to fuck off. One of them protested. He picked up a stick, held it like he meant to cause damage and they all scampered.

He sat back down. Looked at me with: 'Charlie, boy.'

'How's Pookie?'

He was wearing the same tracksuit, same smig, same gold medal around his neck.

'I heard you ran a fella out of Galway for me.'

'That's what we agreed in Athlone.'

'Little prick he was.'

Beat. He took the measure of me, tapping into his Celtic traveller instinct. Somewhere in his heart he decided I was welcome, not here to make trouble, said: 'Tis known you're a man that likes a drink.'

'That'd be right.'

'Will you have a droppa the good stuff?'

'What's the good stuff?'

He took a bottle out from the under the seat, said: 'Poteen.'

He picked up two glasses from the grass, filled them, handed me one, said: 'Always better to drink a right drink if you're goin drinkin at all.'

It was clear, pure, a fermented liquefied diamond. I saluted him and we drank. It was intravenous, straight to the core. Makes the brain sit up, like a tired horse with new life, ready for action. My legs shook, weak with strength of it. We had another, let the spirit dance on our nerves, then got down to business: 'Tell me what has you up in Sligo?'

'Kavanagh.'

'Another bollox.'

'He's tryin to tax us.'

'What for?'

'We're doin some work on the border.'

'He's full of that shit. What you say to him?'

'Nothin yet. What do you reckon?'

He topped us up, said: 'He has some serious boys behind him, but he's not well liked.'

'I'll drink to that.'

He breathed through his nose, asked: 'What does steady Freddie think?'

'He's after gettin arrested.'

'That's not good.'

'Not good at all. What's the problem with you and

Kavanagh?'

'He hates Travellers.'

'That it?'

'And he wanted money for me bringing my trucks down from above, same as yourself. I told him no.'

More Poteen. My tongue liked it. My throat was terrified. I felt home, like this was the one I'd been waiting for.

Pookie continued: 'But the one you have to watch is Lonergan.'

'Lonergan?'

'Let me tell you somethin about Lonergan.'

'Tell me somethin about Lonergan.'

'Lonergan. You can't trust Lonergan.'

'Why not?'

'He's too well in with the shades.'

'So's Freddie?'

'Still, even at that. There's talk.'

'What kinda talk?'

'How come Freddie's arrested? Everythin was set up and goin lovely and next thing…'

'Lonergan is makin a move?'

He drank, rasped, said: 'That's great stuff, boy.' Then: 'That's the way I see it. First Lonergan got rid of McWard, now he has Freddie locked up, and next it'll be you and me and he'll be ready to take it all over. He's usin Joyce and Kavanagh to stir the shit but he's behind it all. I guarantee you. I heard they bust up a girl of yours house below in Salthill? I'd bet that was Lonergan too. Made it look like Paddy Joyce, stirring the shit. And how do you think the fenian found out all about your operations up there? Lonergan's a snake, he is, a pure dirty Dracula, no blood in his body.'

'But he doesn't have the contacts in the west. That's our leverage against him. He's goin nowhere.'

'They'll go where the money is. This is a man that has every port in the country except Galway. McWard was useless, they didn't trust him from the boats. Kramer was a lunatic and they were afraid of him. But what Freddie did is introduce everyone and made himself no good. Why pay him €200,000 a month for nothin? You can give €50,000 straight to the lads bringing it in and they'll cut Freddie loose in two seconds. See what I'm sayin to ya? Then all Lonergan has to do is pay the guards in Galway more than Freddie and he's the main supplier in the whole country and it's adios, boys. Freddie better be careful, or he'll be found hung in a cell somewhere next.'

'Did he try to cut you in?'

'Lonergan? No. He's not my people, and he knows it. You and Freddie I can deal with, but not the likes of him. I know it in his face to look at him, first chance he gets he'll slit my throat.'

'So what now?'

He filled two more, said: 'I've a few ideas.'

'What about Joe Ward?'

'Me and Joe are on the same page. Don't worry about Joe. Let's deal with them other snakes.'

'Will he not be tempted by Lonergan?'

'No, he's one of our own, it's not about the money for Joe. That's where Lonergan is gone wrong. He doesn't understand the west. We're alright til ya break your word, and then we'll never forget, ya can't buy us with two faces. What we need to do is make everyone afraid.'

'How?'

'You saw me holdin that stick to the kids, and they all ran away, why was that?'

'Because you meant it?'

'Exactly. Because I spill blood when it needs to be spilled, and people are nothin but pure animals, and when they smell blood, they'll back off. Same as if they don't smell it, they'll keep comin. It's time to put manners on the whole fuckin lot of them.'

One of the women came over, huge arse, belly, arms, asked: 'Is it you that was with the girl that got killed down in Galway?'

I was afraid she meant Karena, asked: 'El Niño?'

'That's her.'

I drank, said: 'Did ya know her?'

'I heard all about it, god love ya. She looked like a daycent crayture in the pictures on the papers.'

'She was.'

'And them other dogs paid the price too. At least she won't be forgot. Did ya give him a drink, Pookie?'

I held it up, said: 'It's fine stuff.'

'You're welcome here any time. Bring a bottle home with ya.'

And she walked off.

'That's my missus.' Said Pookie. 'Great woman. Tis her father that makes the poteen, that's our test here.'

'What?'

'If you can handle it, you're alright.'

'And what if ya can't?'

'Many's the man be in a hoola hoop after one shot and he wakes up there about five fields over. And the likesa Lonergan wouldn't even make it through the gate. But not you. You're good people, Charlie. You have our backin. The west looks after the west.'

Ultan speaking

The cops raided the flat the next day. I watched from across the road. Drinking poteen, adding fire to my hate. They pulled up, knew exactly where they were going, kicked in the door. No sign of Charlie, they left, deflated. Lonergan was coming for me, no doubt about it. Here's the fella that killed Oscar, and Malone, and Kramer, and Fuzzy and Joey Juju and the other big bollocks that was with him. Looks good for the guards, a big score, let's take him out nice and quietly. Say he resisted arrest, one less scumbag on the street, have the journalists drooling.

Time to make a plan.

I called the accountant, and he didn't answer. That pissed me off. They'd be coming for him too. This is how it would go down. Total wipeout. I wanted my money before they tortured it out of him.

Then he rang back all chirpy with: 'Hello, Ultan speaking?'

Like what the fuck?

'It's Charlie.'

'Oh, hi....'

'How much money can you have in a suitcase tonight?'

'In cash?'

'Yeah.'

'Hmm...how much do you want?'

'Maximum.'

'Max I could have is €300,000. But I'd have to clear it with Freddie.'

'Don't talk to Freddie.'

'I have to.'

'He's in jail. You can't contact him.'

'But…'

'For anythin.'

'I know, but…'

'We can't link you to him. This is for me. Don't fuck it up.'

He let that settle, assembled the future in his confused mind, nervously asked: 'Are you coming here?'

'Yeah.'

'When?'

'Two hours.'

'Two hours?'

'Two hours.'

And I hung up.

Exterior. Outside The Creggan. Athlone. I lit a smoke, pulled in deep, exhaled. Black clouds in the distance. A smell like monoxide. The poteen was wearing off, causing immediate detox. My heart was going sideways, sweats breaking out, a tremor in my hands. I had a quarter of the bottle left and sculled it back, let it calibrate the springs, put the watch back in action.

Then. I needed to get to Galway. The truck didn't have the speed or subtlety required. Decided on a Ford Mondeo. Brand new and black. Spotted the family going into McDonalds and followed them.

Inside, everything was red, and there was a smell like grease and burger sauce mixed with cucumber. Lot of noise and confused queues. He was at the counter, she was in the jacks, and her bag was left on the table with the kids playing on a tablet.

Easy rob.

Outside, breezy reality, the present moment, theft and dopamine.

I went through the bag. The keys weren't in it. Had to go through a load of make-up, small change and a hairbrush. No joy.

Fuck. Threw it on the floor by the door where they'd find it. Took a scan around, spotted a nice Avensis, twenty years old, two-litre. No fancy alarms and easy to hotwire. Went back to the truck and found a screwdriver and got to work.

Ten minutes later I was on the road. Through Ballinasloe, the toll bridge, and sailed to Galway. Great wheels. Good balance, a smell like cigarette ash and old strawberries. Analogue radio playing Today FM. Some pop song, followed by a DJ talking shite. How much to put in a wedding card, pitfalls when buying a house, a date that went wrong, all the big problems. Time for the news then.

The feud made the headlines.

Serious police operation planned for the weekend. An arrest warrant out for a known criminal known as Charlie, wanted in connection with a series of crimes. Considered armed and dangerous, do not approach.

Christ, I was fuckin famous. Lonergan must be paying them big money. Drank the last of poteen and threw the bottle out the window. There was a scared smash of scattered glass as I came in by the clinic and found Ultan's place.

Interior. Shithole office. Night.

He was in a black jacket, black tie, blue shirt, clean shaven.

Gelled hair. Soft hands. He was nervous, like he was unsure about the quality of his homework. I said: 'How are ya fixed?'

He took a suitcase from under the table, said: 'I got what you asked.'

'Good.'

'But I really need to talk to Freddie.'

'I told you. Don't.'

'I'm worried. You and Freddie are all over the news. This is a lot more exposure than I asked for.'

'Who're ya tellin?'

I opened the case. It looked good. Enough.

Ultan asked: 'What now?'

'Some people are going to come here and try to kill you.'

'What? Who?'

'Does it really matter?'

'Oh my God. What should I do?'

'I'll see ya round.'

And I left.

Back in Athlone. Burnt the car at the Battery Heights. Felt bad, like I was destroying a piece of the decent past. But I couldn't have them finding it, checking for fingerprints, tracking my movements to Ultan's place and back here again.

Walked back over the bridge. Could hear the sirens of the fire brigade. The poteen shakes were kicking in. Bought a bottle of Jim Beam in O'Brien's to take the edge off. Slept in the truck. Dreamt of Karena. Her voice saying I was no good, a wasteland, but there was hope in her tone, like I could prove her wrong.

Woke up stiff and dehydrated. The sun coming in the windscreen, like mockery. I let down the window down. Everything was clear and calm.

I took a swig of the bourbon and rang Kavanagh. He answered all proud, said: 'Yes, sir?'

'I'll have a truck waiting for you today.'

'Nice that you saw sense.'

'It's a depot in Athlone.'

'Tiger Tony's place? We know all about it. Where's my twenty grand?'

'It'll be waiting for you in Mountbellew. How's three o'clock?'

'Three o'clock it is.'

Next stop Woodies.

Walked in, the dominant colour was green. A smell like sawdust and mothballs. Long aisles of paint, carpet and plants. Couples and families shopping for kitchens, barbecues, and insulation. Wandering around like glassy eyed innocent dreamers.

Eventually found the tools section.

Scanned around.

Hacksaw was a bit dramatic. Chainsaw would be too Columbian. There was pliers, bolt cutters, vice grips. I settled on a wire cutter, subtle but effective. Bought that, left again, into the roaring noon.

Time for another car, but I was sick of stealing them, and the attention wasn't worth it. Spotted a Civic for sale on the Dublin Road. Rang the number. A girl called Shauna leaving for Australia tomorrow, looking for a quick deal.

She wanted €1500

I offered a €1000.

She came down to €1300.

Job done. She said she'd be there in ten minutes.

Twenty minutes later, she arrived in the passenger seat of a blue BMW. Probably the boyfriend driving. Earring, pasty young face, mullet. Looked like a pissed off apprentice mechanic.

Shauna hopped out. Pink fleece, grey jeggings, blonde hair. Holding an iPhone.

Chirpy voice, she said: 'Hi!'

I was smoking on the bonnet, said: 'Howya.'

She got uncertain, like this mightn't be safe. Looked back to make sure your man was still there. He was, head down, scanning through his phone, not interested.

I took out the money, rolled off thirteen notes, handed them to her, said: 'This should do it.'

She did a quick count, handed me the keys and the logbook, said: 'Perfect thanks. I have everything here.'

I made up a fake name, address, gave it back to her, said: 'Good luck in Australia.'

'Thanks, sorry it took me so long to get here. There's a lot of checkpoints around.'

I played casual, asked her: 'Where'd ya come from?'

'Coosan, there's guards everywhere, some kind of gang thing.'

I lit another smoke, said: 'Awful.'

She hesitated, like she recognised me, might ask an awkward question, then held out a €100 and said: 'Here.'

'What's that?'

'For luck. It's the way my dad always did a sale.'

'Tell him thanks, but it's already a good deal, no need.'

'He's not around anymore, but you remind me of him a

little bit.'

'Will you not need it for Australia?'

'Please, it'll make me feel better.'

I took it. She was pleased, like a nun taking a compliment, her green eyes brighter, like she passed a test. Your man in the Beamer looked up, asked: 'Are ya right?'

'I better go. I still have to pack. Good luck with everything. Take the bypass if you want to avoid the checkpoints.'

Your man pulled wheelspins as they left, leaving black tracks and the smell of burnt rubber on the road.

Used the luck money for cans and faced for Dublin.

The interior of the car was fresh. Strong smell of perfume and make-up. There was a slight crack on the windscreen but otherwise it ran perfect and had the right amount of low profile. Innocent white, N plate on the back, pink dice on the rearview mirror.

Buzzed past Moate, Tullamore, Mullingar, Kinnegad, Enfield.

Followed the arteries into the city. Took a right for Southbound and the exit for Dundrum.

Found the nice house in the suburbs, just like Pookie told me.

I parked up. Lit a smoke, drank cans, let David Bowie through the speakers with *Fall Dog Bombs the Moon.*

A light drizzle started, bounced on the window, obscured the view until I hit the wipers. That's when Joyce pulled up on his motorbike. Same jacket, same earring, boyband hair style. He got off, left the helmet on the seat, and went inside. I gave it five minutes, let him settle, then made my way over.

Vauxhaul Cavalier

Back in Athlone. Needed something to line the stomach, stop me puking blood and bile. Found a Kebab House.

The dominant colour was red.

Indian lads working.

Went with a lamb doner and chips.

Ate it in the car across the road from Tiger Tony's place. Had a perfect view of the tanks, the trucks, the entrance and exit.

Kavanagh arrived early. Wasn't hard to spot the yellow Northern registration on the Vauxhall Cavalier. Window down, thick hand on the steering wheel, bullshit tattoos. He pulled in like he knew all about it. Took a spin around and parked beside the taps.

He got out. White vest, stomach hanging down, blue jeans, sunglasses. Superior attitude. Like he could tidy up a few things if he had the chance. Another lad came out of the passenger side. Skinned head, thin black jeans, concave stomach, nose rings, thick boots. Looked like a mangy dog on heroin. Kavanagh gave him the keys and he drove the car away.

The truck was in the usual spot. He walked over. Checked it out, kicked the tyres and got in, turned the ignition, and left.

I rang Pookie, ethereal halting site noise in the background. Wind, a symphony of loud voices, dogs barking. I said: 'That fella's after leavin here.'

He was calm, sure, said: 'We'll be waitin. Did you find that other place?'

'I did.'

'Good man.'

Click.

Exterior. Tullamore. Evening. Lonergan lived in a big estate called Arden Hills. Big gardens. Tall trees. All cars up to date. Looked like a place for doctors, vets, politicians. Old money.

His house was down the back. Secluded big gate. Needed a code to get in but otherwise no security. He was too arrogant to think the likes of me could find him, but Pookie had eyes everywhere, knowing a day like this would come.

Lonergan's car wasn't there. Figured I'd drink another can and watch the place for a while. Smoked a Benson, let the music glide through Shauna's ex-radio. The Clash were singing *Should I stay or should I go?*

A blonde girl arrived. Sunglasses, tight black jeans, pink headband. She was walking a small terrier. They paused at the gate. She took her time entering the code - 7337 - then disappeared inside. I gave it half an hour. Had no more cans left so I drank a half bottle of Jameson. Then it was dark and I said fuck this, she might know where the fucker is.

It was cold now, too. And quiet. Each house was like a social fortress. Trees around the gardens, nobody looking over your wall. Nobody wondering why Charlie was here.

Typed in the code. Heard a confirmed click and the gate opened. Inside, cobbled stone, a fountain with a naked angel and a big brown door. I pressed the bell.

She answered, holding a phone, looked me up and down, asked: 'Yeah?'

Pale green eyes. 'I'm lookin for John.'

'Dad?'

'Yeah, is he about?'

'Why?'

'He asked me to call.'

'How did you get in the gate?'

'He gave me the code and asked me to wait - 7337?'

This reassured her and she said: 'What's your name? I'll call him.'

'Tell him it's Paddy Joyce.'

'Ok, Paddy. Do you want to come in?'

She pulled back the door. I walked in. Long hallway. Tile floors. A modem flashing to the right. Wedding pictures on the walls. A smell like carbolic soap. Into the kitchen. Island counter. Bright, shiny taps. Tall fridge. Music on, The Rolling Stones *Ruby Tuesday.*

"Lose your dreams and you will lose your mind, ain't life unkind?"

She turned it down, said: 'I'm Gemma. Do you work for dad?'

'Occasionally. He's a busy man.'

'He certainly is.'

'Nice house.'

'It's ok. I actually live in Maynooth. I'm just visiting for the day.'

She had the phone to her ear, said: 'Dad isn't answering. You can call back if you don't want to wait?'

There was a hint of regret in her tone, like she was lonely. I said: 'I suppose I can.'

'Or I was just about to have a joint if you fancy it?'

'I'll take a whisky if it's goin?'

'Dad has loads. Stick around. I get anxiety when I'm alone.'

She left. Came back with a bottle of Jameson. Filled me a tumbler. I noticed a tremor in her hands and a sparkling diamond on her finger.

'Ring looks new?'

She looked at it sceptically, like a bad car she got talked into buying. 'That? It's ok. It's an engagement ring.'

'Congratulations.'

'I wish. Last thing I want to do is get married.'

'You're goin a strange way about it.'

'I'm not designed for monogamy. I don't even know why I said YES. Social pressure I think. We're both teachers and just fell into it.'

'What are you goin to do?'

'I don't know. I can't tell anyone. It's too far gone. Wedding's in a month. And we just bought a house for half a million.'

She thought of herself, looked at me, said: 'Sorry, I'm nervous.'

'What's there to be nervous about?'

She rolled the joint, said: 'Nothing, I suppose. It's nice to say these things out loud. How's your whisky?'

'Like smoky wet timber.'

She lit up, it was corporeal, asked: 'So what do you really want with my dad?'

'We have business issues to iron out.'

'I know what he does - like what he *really* does. Are you a dealer?'

'No.'

'I just got out of rehab last week, a victim of my father's success. How's that for irony?'

'It definitely qualifies.'

'International drug dealer dedicates his life to having the perfect daughter and she ends up being a junkie.'

'So you're not a teacher?'

'I'm on sick leave. I got high with a student. Then I fucked him in the male toilets.'

Her green eyes danced, judging my reaction. She still had the headband on, her blonde hair pushed back. Her face was oily, unblemished, like there was a hidden hormone making her shine.

'Does the fiancé know?'

'About the rehab? Yeah. My dad had the rest covered up.'

'But you're still engaged, with a house for half a million?'

'And I thought Oxycontin would make it all go away.'

'Does the weed help?'

'Slows me down enough to get through the day.'

'Your problems are imaginary. You could just walk away.'

'I could, couldn't I? But where would I go? I'm in a cage of invisible bars. There's no escaping yourself.'

Beat, she watched me through the smoke, then asked: 'So why did you lie?'

'About what?'

'I know Paddy Joyce. And you're not him.'

'There could be more than one Paddy Joyce.'

'And I saw you sitting outside before I came in. Is that how you got the code?'

'Yeah.'

'And your face was on the news for killing somebody in Galway.'

'Does that bother you?'

She thought, said: 'No. I find it exciting.'

'You're not afraid?'

'I'm so dead inside I'd take fear just to feel alive.'

That's when Lonergan arrived. Grey hair, suit, pale, rheumy eyes. He was shocked to see me, drinking in his kitchen, with his daughter getting stoned. He went for authority, with: 'What the fuck are you doin here?'

He was already reaching for a weapon inside his jacket. I wasted no time, hit him over the head with the glass. It smashed and cut him open at the forehead. He yelped like a kicked dog. Gemma screamed as we fell on the floor, like two UFC fighters in a complicated lock. Stools fell and clattered on the tiles. He was stronger than he looked, but I got him under control.

He was panting, wheezing, spitting blood.

I kept it simple. Took out the Glock, took aim, said: 'Any last words?'

He looked up at me, calculating, the sly algorithms scanning for mercy, sympathy, a ticket out. 'Not in front of her.'

'Fuck yourself.'

And I pulled the trigger. The kitchen had never heard anything like it. The pictures, vases, cookbooks, scarred for life.

Gemma was statuesque, mouth open, the joint still in her hand, not even half smoked. Something had broken inside her. She had transferred to a new level of despair and the bridge back had collapsed.

'Daddy?' She said, then looked at me. 'Tell him to wake up.'

'I'm sorry.'

'What did you do?'

'Maybe this is your way out.'

And I raised the gun.

Galway Blues

The papers didn't know what the fuck to do. Lonergan and his daughter found dead. Kavanagh's body found in a ditch in Brideswell. And Paddy Joyce paraplegic in a rehab centre in Dundrum. Seems he was on the Suzuki and hit a truck on the M50. Terrible that. I bought a card in Mr. Price and sent it up to him.

> *Get well soon, Paddy.*
> *Best wishes, Charlie.*
> *(p.s. I hope there's better brakes on the wheelchair)*

Pookie was right about one thing. People were afraid. Oscar's woman dropped the charges. Said the daughter was mixed up with the time I stayed there. Lovely man really, gave them a grand going out the door and they never saw me again.

And the cops had to let Freddie go. They had no proof of anything and every witness was too terrified to talk. They even gave him back the box of magnets. Nobody wanted to be on the bad side of us. With Lonergan gone, they knew we were in charge, and not to be fucked with. I was on the way down to pick him up but first I had to stop at Tommy Ryan's to make a collection. I parked at the house in Roscommon and walked in. He was in the kitchen. Bright but dilapidated, no feminine touch. He was thinner, sicker, I said: 'Alright, Tommy?'

'Cut-throat Charlie himself.'

'What's that supposed to mean?'

'That's what the papers are calling you now. Should I have rolled out the red carpet?'

'You got my money?'

He left a suitcase on the counter. 'I have it here. Cash.'

'How much?'

'€400,000.'

'That'll do.'

'Forty stacks of €10,000. I still owe Freddie a hundred so it's €300,000 clear.'

'That's €300,000 divided by three then.'

'How do you mean?'

'We'll split the profit. Take €90,000, I'll give €90,000 to Freddie plus his €100,000 back and I'll take €120,000 cos I'm doin all the drivin.'

'Serious?'

'A cut's a cut.'

His eyes dilated, like he had a home for it already: 'Cheltenham starts today. I was only lookin at it this morning.'

'Do whatever you want.'

'Thanks, Charlie. Nobody's done a decent thing for me in a long time.'

I pulled out a contract, said: 'You better sign this too.'

'What's that?'

'The banks are almost paid. This is a transfer of ownership to us when you die.'

'Seriously?'

'I'm not askin here. And I'm in a hurry. I'll split the profits with ya until then.'

He looked at the ninety grand, said: 'To hell with it. Give me the biro.'

He signed, then asked: 'Will you drop me at the bookies? The Ford is out of petrol. I've a tip for a horse too if you want it. *Galway Blues.* It's a sure thing. I'll tell you all about it on the way.'

The wheels of justice

Have faith in Christ and all her sisters. Drink inspired random phrases, like data packets or snatched radio waves, grazing across my frazzled mind. I came into Galway through a haze of emotional stigmata. El Niño here, Karena there. A blanket of guilt on a bed of regret. Silently losing grip, all things dying, the rope slipping through my drunk hands. A life designed to create the uncreation. A bottle of Jack Daniels to deaden the shakes, to keep the picture steady.

I picked up Freddie at Mill Street. He walked out, blue jeans, Che Guevara t-shirt, the makings of a beard. He sat in, smelled like old socks, said: 'Fuck sake.'

'Free at last.'

'Now I know how Mandela felt.' He lit a smoke, inhaled hard, said: 'The guards don't know what to make of it.'

'Last time they'll deal with an outsider like Lonergan.'

'Fuckin hope so.'

'And Pookie is in town. He's over at the pub. Wants to meet and pay what he owes.'

'That'll do. Face her for Forster Street.'

Exterior. *The Galway Hooker.* It had a new blue door and shiny windows. Cally was there. Black leather jacket, keeping an eye on things. He shook my hand, said: 'Great to have ya back.'

'The wheels of justice move slow.'

Inside. Smell of bleach, and paint, and club sandwiches. Televisions going. Golf, soccer, world news. Pink Floyd with

Another Brick in the Wall.

No dark sarcasm in the classroom.

The renovation gave the place a more modern look. Funky stools, ambient lighting, an extension with a huge screen for watching sports. Didn't matter. It was empty without Karena. Like a jigsaw with a vital piece missing.

Pookie sat at the counter drinking Smithwicks and watching racing on the telly. He turned around, said: 'Alright boys?'

'How's Poo*keen*?'

'Good man, Freddie.'

'Are ya long waitin?'

'I'm alright. Killed the time backin horses.'

'You have a present for me?'

'I do. Somewhere quiet we can open it?'

There was an alcove down the back. Perfect for a private chat. Pookie had the money in a holdall.

Freddie unzipped it, said: 'What's there?'

'A straight million.'

'Add it up for me.'

'Back taxes for me and Joe while you were inside and a bit of the other stuff.'

'What's the other stuff?'

'Way I see it I can still do Galway for the gear and ye do everythin else. Joe Ward moves into the midlands and takes over Lonergan's patch and me and him have contacts in Dublin that'll fill the hole left by Paddy the wank. I can handle the action from the North through Fermanagh so I'll make up Kavanagh's tax and you don't suffer.'

Freddie closed it up, said: 'I love it when a plan comes together.'

'We got lucky this time, but there'll be other cunts comin. There always is. If it wasn't for Charlie, it could have gone another way entirely.'

'I hear ya. Let's keep the lines of communication open. Any threats, we'll get them squashed before they grow fangs.'

Pookie finished his pint, said: 'West takes care of the west, boys. We stick by that, nathin'll break us.'

A cold wave came over me, like I got shot with a million tiny arrows. Time for a stronger drink.

Went to the bar to get a round. Had a Jim Beam chaser while waiting for the pints.

Noticed *The Sunday Times Magazine* on the counter. The headline caught my eye. *Local Talent Shines as Gang Feud Goes to Hollywood.*

Karena's blue eyes bounced off the page. The article said it was her best performance to date. Oscar nominated. She had brought authenticity to the role. Captured the underworld with devastating accuracy. It was a whole feature. How she prepared for the part. What it took, what she put herself through. She had known the story through personal experience. Always felt compelled to capture it. Like it was her destiny as an artist. She was born to resurrect the character and immortalize her on screen. To give meaning to a life cut short by tragedy. Her process meant she had to understand the protagonist at every level. Dress like her, dye her hair, take on her accent, her mannerisms, the way she walked. Drink the same drink, wear the same perfume, live in the same environment. She rented a house in Salthill. Stocked it with the books and music her heroine liked. Got a job in a Galway pub connected to a local gang. Observed conversations, connections, routines. Struck up a relationship with a well-known criminal. Mined him for information. Even lived with him for a while. Picked up on illegal operations, scams. Money laundering, debt collecting, intimidation. Gained insights into his social history. Stunned by the levels of juvenile delinquency. The abuse at industrial schools around the country. Often felt conflicted, in too deep. Too much sympathy with the monsters in the material. Eager to stress the motivations and duality of the legally deviant mind. Publicly they break the law, but what are the private reasons for doing it? Do they know themselves? What are the addicts and recidivists trying to work through? The film touches on this but comes down on the side of the tragedy she captured, the life she celebrated, and the memory she preserved.

Needed intense therapy to emerge as her true self. Find her way back. And there she was. Her hair blonde again. She was living in her LA home with her American co-star who is also her long-time partner. They had worked on the film for over a year. She wrote it. He had the Hollywood connections to get it picked up and produced. Same fella I saw talking to her on video call at the kitchen table. They planned to get married soon. He understood her art, her methods, and didn't feel any jealously for her recent infidelities. *"All part of the role..."*

I turned the page and read more. Too many women killed in Ireland. Jean McConville. Veronica Guerin. Aisling Murphy. She was sick of it. Especially the recent attack on a young girl (Sharon O'Malley) during a robbery in a Topaz petrol station. The brutality and horrific injuries inspired her to bring the timeline for the project forward and be more ambitious and determined than ever to highlight the madness. The risk a woman takes just leaving the house every day. She wanted to help all women rise and be confident and champion change, promote a society where it was safe to walk down the street. Go for a run. Do your job. To never feel ashamed, threatened, scared or less valuable. And not be a prop in the theatre of narcissistic men.

Pookie shouted over to the guy behind the bar: 'Hey, did *Galway Blues* come in?'

'No. Still fuckin runnin.'

Did she feel guilty about betraying her lover? The

duplicity and deceit? No, the work was too important, and she couldn't dilute her role in exchange for personal feelings. She regards herself as a different woman then, a different person. At its height and most intense, her feelings did become conflicted and confused but in hindsight she realizes she got out just in time. She narrowly missed getting shot in a botched assassination attempt, her home was attacked by thugs, and recently there was the killing of John Lonergan's innocent daughter. Let's not forget she had a name. It was Gemma.

Despite her wider social goals and aspirations, does she think she did justice to the story? Yes, she hopes. She revived a life that was getting lost in the media obsession with cartel crime and high-profile personalities that inadvertently celebrates violent males. The audience needs to decide if she succeeded, but she jokes that the Oscar nod helps.

'Hey, Charlie, where's them fuckin pints?'

'Gimme a minute.'

I read on. Have the police talked to her about what she knows?

Not yet, but she won't tell them anything. She's an artist. Not an undercover cop. Same as a journalist never reveals her sources. (Saying that, there's nothing to stop them watching the film themselves and pursuing anything they find credible.) For her, she hopes she brought acting to a new level, a standard to aspire to, with the power to effect change through reconstruction of the social mindset towards women in Ireland and beyond. For now she needs time to focus on herself and fully rebuild. On a lighter note, what's her preferred eye colour? She likes the natural blue and is glad to be finished with the brown contact lenses as they irritated her eyes. But sometimes she looks in the mirror and her heart breaks, and she cries as her other self fades, and she prays she hasn't failed.

The pints came. I paid and finished the article while waiting for the change. It was the last line that really got me.

Nearly knocked me off the stool.
> The title of the film.
> *El Niño.*

ACKNOWLEDGEMENT

Special thanks to *Mayo County Council Arts Office* for their continued and invaluable support and especially for making this book possible.

BOOKS BY THIS AUTHOR

El Niño

Set in Galway City, in the rugged heart of Ireland's West, El Niño begins when Charlie, a recovering alcoholic and seasoned pickpocket, steals El Niño's wallet – then falls in love with her. A passionate affair follows and threatens the delicate sober balance he has fought hard to maintain. Then. A chance encounter with one of Kramer's crew—his old friend and former partner in crime—complicates matters further. When the crew offers him a high-stakes job, the pressure mounts, pulling him deeper into the criminal underworld he's been desperately trying to escape.

Could this one last heist help him and El Niño escape Galway for good – or will it be their ultimate undoing? In the vein of gritty dramas like City of God, Narcos, and Love/Hate, El Niño blends intense romance with brutal realities, capturing the volatile tension between love and survival. Against the stark beauty of Ireland's West, this dark and edgy novel explores passion, loyalty, and the price of freedom. With crisp, biting dialogue and a narrative style reminiscent of Ken Bruen, Declan Burke, and Lee Child, El Niño vividly depicts Galway's vibrant streets and seedy underbelly. Showcasing the storytelling talent of screenwriter and playwright Mick Donnellan, it's a gripping tale of obsession, betrayal, and the weight of impossible choices. The reader will be left stunned by a twist ending that challenges everything they thought they knew. www.mickdonnellan.com

BOOKS BY THIS AUTHOR

Fisherman's Blues

A Darkly Comic Thrill Ride through the West of Ireland Underworld, Where Romance, Crime, and Sharp Wit Collide.

"Mick Donnellan is the new Tarantino." Florence Films.

"A unique voice in the west" Irish Theatre Magazine.

"Voice of the new generation." Electric Picnic.

Jack, recently cut off the dole, lands a job at a shady telesales centre in Galway, only to find it's a front for a timeshare scam. Life takes an unexpected turn when he begins a passionate affair with Dyane, a sharp-witted customer, and dives into Galway's vibrant pub scene alongside his boss, Chris. But their carefree nights take a sinister twist when a washed-up private investigator, Jennings, starts digging into the scam. Soon, Dyane and two other women vanish, forcing Jack, Chris, and Jennings into a desperate search. As their ties to Galway's criminal underworld deepen, the once-wild Irish melodies take on a haunting note, reflecting their dangerous descent.

Music and Irish lyrics flow through the story, with the poetic strains of "Fisherman's Blues" by The Waterboys weaving throughout, capturing the wild, untamed spirit of the Irish coast and the unpredictable lives of its characters. The song echoes through the narrative, hinting that it might hold answers to the mysteries unfolding—its lyrics becoming a refuge that lingers in Jack's mind as he searches for meaning in the chaos around him. With flavours reminiscent of Martin McDonagh's sharp wit, Ken Bruen's gritty crime, Mike McCormack's lyrical storytelling, and Flann O'Brien's surreal humour, this tale is both uniquely Irish and universally gripping.

From the mind of acclaimed playwright Mick Donnellan, Fisherman's Blues weaves a gripping tale of love, friendship, and danger. Be prepared for a uniquely Irish thriller that lingers long after the final page.

"Reminiscent of Joyce, with a modern slant." Irish Cultural Centre of Denmark.

www.mickdonnellan.com

BOOKS BY THIS AUTHOR

The Naked Flame

The Naked Flame is Mick Donnellan's electrifying fourth novel, a gripping tale of love, betrayal, and the dangerous allure of desire. John-joe is engaged to be married, but he's plagued by doubts he can't ignore. Uncertain how to break things off with his fiancée Karen, everything changes when he meets the irresistible Marilyn during a wild stag night in Madrid. Their steamy encounter sets off a chain of events that spirals out of control: the wedding is abruptly canceled, John-joe becomes a suspect in a double murder, and mysterious calls urge him to come to London.

As John-joe is thrust into a surreal world teeming with unusual characters and perilous choices, he's left with no one to trust except the enigmatic Marilyn, who seems to hold all the answers—but at a potentially devastating cost. Set in Athlone, the heart of the Irish midlands, The Naked Flame weaves an erotic and thrilling narrative rich with both dark humor and poignant tragedy. With unexpected twists and a heart-stopping climax, this novel captures the wild unpredictability of life and love, leaving readers breathless until the very last page.

www.mickdonnellan.com

BOOKS BY THIS AUTHOR

The Dead Soup: Controlling Their Minds Is Much Simpler.

Discover the heart and soul of Ireland in this award-winning collection of short stories, set against the stunning landscapes of the West and the hidden corners of the midlands. From the rugged hills of Ballinrobe to the bustling streets of Galway City and Athlone, each story pulls you into a world where the raw realities of Irish life unfold. Meet unforgettable characters—alcoholic guards, cunning landlords, bigoted locals, and a vibrant cast of scammers and misfits—brought to life through Donnellan's trademark razor-sharp dialogue and keen, unflinching observations. These tales blend love, addiction, and the darkly humorous spirit of Irish tragedy, offering a deeply moving, thought-provoking journey that will leave you both laughing and reflecting long after the final page. A must-read for those who crave stories that resonate with authenticity and heart.

www.mickdonnellan.com

Printed in Great Britain
by Amazon